# Dollhouse of the Dead

Look for the next exciting title in
THE GHOST IN THE DOLLHOUSE series:

#2 *The Headless Bride*

## Dollhouse of the Dead

Kathryn Reiss

SCHOLASTIC INC.
New York Toronto London Auckland Sydney

ISBN 0-590-60360-4



12 11 10 9 8 7 6 5 4 3 2 1 7 8 9/9 0 1 2/0

Printed in the U.S.A. 40
First Scholastic printing, March 1997

Thanks to Mary Beth Faustine, Susan Ito,
and Janet Johnson for their time, talk, and talents
as I worked on shaping this story . . .

and thanks especially to my husband, Tom Strychacz,
for once more believing, brainstorming —
and being there with tea when I needed it.

*This book is for our son*
*Nicholas Graham,*
*who would know a ghost if he saw one.*

# Dollhouse of the Dead

# Chapter 1

There were three reasons Zibby Thorne should be happy. Today was the first day of summer vacation, with weather just perfect for Rollerblading — sunny and fresh and not too muggy. She had done well on her report card, too — even managed to pass French, her very worst subject — and so she had a very proud and relieved mom and was also now officially a sixth-grader. And today was her eleventh birthday.

But Zibby wasn't happy at all. And there were three reasons for that, too. The first was that sunny summer days didn't matter since Amy, her very best friend in all the world since they were three years old, had moved away. It had shocked both girls that the move couldn't even wait till the last day of school. But Amy's parents' new jobs demanded that they be in their new city immediately. The new city was Cleveland, horrible and big — at least that's what Amy had reported by phone the night they arrived — and hours and hours away from Carroway. The second reason was that the same mail delivery that had brought her report card also brought a postcard from her dad. Not even a real letter, though Zibby had written to him three times in the past month. The postcard had a picture of a boat called a gondola and had been sent from Italy over a week ago announcing that he and Sofia had been married. Finally, even though it was Zibby's birthday and her mom had promised they could go to Sportsmart and buy new Rollerblades, her mom had dragged her all the way to Columbus — the closest city to Carroway — to go to a miniature show.

And so that's where they were. Zibby hadn't even known what a miniature show was. Now she knew more than she ever wanted to know. They'd been here in the vast convention hall for hours, it seemed, looking at dolls, miniature furnishings for miniature houses, and even the miniature stuff people used to build the houses: shingles and bricks and boards. Zibby loved building things and was a good carpenter, but she had been interested in the tiny bricks and boards for only about ten minutes. What could you build with such tiny bricks except a tiny chimney for a dollhouse? And she didn't have a dollhouse and didn't want one. She wanted Rollerblades.

She stood in one corner of the huge convention center ballroom, nibbling a cookie (*not* a miniature one, fortunately), watching. Her mom and Aunt Linnea and cousin Charlotte hadn't even wanted to shop for a snack and were only reluctantly taking a ten-minute break from *oohing* and *aahing* over the booths set up everywhere. Soon they'd be out of this place and Zibby'd have her Rollerblades. She was going to buy knee pads and wrist guards, too, because her mom insisted. Her mom insisted she wear a helmet, too, but Zibby already had a bike helmet. She'd been roller-skating for years on an old pair of standard four-wheels handed down from Amy's big sister. But on Rollerblades she'd *fly!*

Zibby had been saving up her allowance to buy the Rollerblades. And with the money her grandparents had given her for her birthday, she had a total of eighty-five dollars. It seemed a vast amount of money to be carrying around in her pocket. But soon, very soon, she'd be handing it over to the clerk at Sportsmart and going home with her new skates — if they ever got out of the miniature show.

Aunt Linnea was the real problem. Collecting tiny, exquisitely handcrafted writing desks with drawers that really opened, teeny four-poster beds with lace canopies, and little pots and pans for a dollhouse kitchen was Aunt Linnea's hobby. She had a miniature house that took up one full corner of their formal dining room. It was, Aunt Linnea had told Zibby, a replica of a famous English stately home called Blickling Hall. Aunt Linnea went to miniature shows like this one all around the country. Now Zibby's mom was becoming interested in miniatures, too. The two of them could easily be here, browsing and buying, until midnight — or whenever the convention center closed.

"I'm so bored, I could die," groaned Zibby, sinking onto a bench along the wall. "Can't I just go to Sportsmart by myself and meet you back at the car when this is over?"

Nell Thorne frowned at her daughter. Zibby already knew what she'd say. And sure enough . . . "Zibby, I'm not going to allow a ten-year-old — okay, an *eleven*-year-old — to roam around a strange city by herself. Now stop fussing."

Well, at least her mom remembered it was her birthday.

"We'll leave soon," Nell was promising, her attention already turned away from Zibby and back to the colorful bustle of the miniature show. "As soon as I look at the dollhouse exhibit."

"How about if Charlotte comes to Sportsmart with me?" pressed Zibby. She didn't really want to go anywhere with her cousin, but it would be better than having to hang around the convention hall.

"I don't want to come with you," Charlotte retorted.

"Charlotte is enjoying herself. You might, too, if you weren't determined to have a bad day." This was said by Aunt Linnea, Charlotte's mother. Aunt Linnea was carrying two tote bags filled with the precious miniature furniture she had bought at the show. She frowned at Zibby.

Zibby took a deep breath. She liked Aunt Linnea most of the time, and didn't really want a fight. "It's just that I didn't want a party or anything," she said softly. "Just Rollerblades."

Zibby's mom put her hand on her daughter's head and brushed back the straight, reddish-gold hair that fell in Zibby's eyes. "Poor birthday girl. Look, give me another fifteen minutes, and then we'll leave." She looked over at her sister. "I'm nearly through here. How about you?"

Aunt Linnea pursed her lips. All around them crowds of miniature enthusiasts surged up and down the aisles of the convention hall, stopping at all the booths to admire the tiny handmade furniture. A whole section of the hall was roped off to display the antique and modern houses for sale. "I suppose I could be ready to go soon," Aunt Linnea said reluctantly. "But not until I've seen the dollhouses. We've saved the best for last and I don't want to miss anything. Some of those houses are museum quality."

Zibby snorted as she watched her aunt walk toward the dollhouse section. "I can't believe Aunt Linnea hasn't run out of money yet, Mom. Have you seen the price tags on some of the things she's bought today? And now she'll spend hundreds of bucks more on a clock only six inches high." Zibby shook her head. "Must be nice to be rich."

"You're just being a pain because your precious Amy is gone," hissed Charlotte behind her. "But I don't see why you should take it out on us. And anyway, I don't say mean things about *your* mom, so you shouldn't say things about *mine.*"

Zibby flushed. "Sorry," she said shortly.

She didn't really mean to be rude. Aunt Linnea and Uncle David were both kind and generous people, and had been especially helpful to Nell and Zibby when Zibby's dad moved out almost two years ago. At first he was just going on a month-long business trip to Italy to help his company set up a branch there. But the month had turned into six months, and the plan for Nell and Zibby to join him had come to nothing once he'd met the Italian woman named Sofia and fallen in love. Zibby couldn't believe it — and still couldn't believe it, even now that the postcard had come, announcing the awful news. She couldn't believe her mom's reaction to the postcard either. Nell had just read it and shrugged her shoulders. "I'm not surprised, honey," was all she said. "I saw this coming for a long, long time. Even before Dad went to Italy in the first place. Don't blame Sofia."

But Zibby had seen nothing coming, and she did blame the unknown Sofia. She had been waiting for them to be a family again and now they wouldn't be. It had to be someone's fault.

She started following her mom across the convention hall, but stopped abruptly as the room seemed to turn in a dizzy whirl. She thought she heard a bell clanging nearby as she staggered against a booth for support. *Whoa!* she thought. Was she coming down with a sudden flu? *I can't be sick on my birthday,* she thought in protest.

Then the room steadied and the bell stopped ringing. Zibby scanned the crowd for her mom. Instead, her gaze fell upon a woman in a gray dress, walking toward the dollhouse exhibit. Zibby set off after her. *Why am I following this woman?* she wondered, and then she laughed. "I know why," she said aloud. "Because it's time for a change." Then she wondered what she meant by that.

She crossed the room behind the woman in gray. The noise in the convention hall was deafening. Zibby glanced around her as she walked — what *was* it she was looking for? — and then stopped so abruptly that the people behind her bumped into her. She barely noticed. *It's time for a change,* she thought again. And there, just ahead, was what she had been looking for.

# Chapter 2

Zibby found herself at the far end of the convention hall, which looked like a little neighborhood made up of houses in all sorts of architectural styles: Georgian manor houses with tiny ivy plants climbing the brick; Victorian mansions with tower rooms and wraparound porches; country farmhouses; city town houses; Swiss chalets, one-room schoolhouses; even a modern geodesic dome house. Zibby felt excited, as if at last it really was her birthday after all.

"It's time for a change," she whispered to herself, walking past all the fine houses on display and stopping at the far corner in front of a big brown-shingled dollhouse with a roof and a front porch even more rickety than the one on her own, real house. It had a front door with a dirty panel of real stained glass. There were three stories and a tower. Unlike the other dollhouses, this one was closed up so that the little rooms inside could not be viewed. And unlike the other dollhouses, this one was filthy. It was covered with dirt and dust and cobwebs.

But it was exactly what she had been looking for.

Zibby reached out a tentative finger and touched one of the little tower windows. Her finger came away grimy. She looked closer. For a second it seemed as if something gray flickered inside — as if something were moving inside the house. She looked more closely, but the little windows were all so dirty it was impossible to see through them. *It isn't anything,* she told herself. Possibly a mouse had gnawed a hole through a wall and was using the house as his private mansion. Good luck to him.

She began to turn away when a bell started clanging close by. She couldn't see who was ringing it. The people milling around didn't seem to hear it. No one turned as she had, wondering where the sound came from. No one else put their hands up to cover their ears against the bell's insistent peal. Then, with a start, Zibby realized that holding her hands over her ears did nothing to shut out the noise. In fact, the ringing seemed to intensify. She removed her hands, then clapped them back over her ears — sure enough, the ringing was louder. It seemed to be inside her head.

She shook her head vigorously. The bell stopped. She took a deep breath and looked around for her mom. With relief, she spotted Nell with Aunt Linnea and Charlotte by a huge dollhouse castle. She hurried over, noting the tags on the dollhouses she passed: *British, circa 1920. Completely furnished, $8,000. American, circa 1940. $4,000. French, electrified, circa 1895. $10,000.*

Zibby felt confused, still dizzy. She tried to ignore the old dollhouse. She tried to concentrate on what her mom, aunt, and cousin were talking about. Charlotte was begging Aunt Linnea for a house that looked like a castle. As if she didn't already have a beautiful dollhouse up in her bedroom.

"Oh, Zib, look at this one," cried Nell, pulling Zibby to the front of the four-foot tall castle Charlotte was going crazy over. "Can you believe it? Wouldn't it be heavenly to build something like this together?"

Zibby hated the wistful note in her mom's voice. It made her feel guilty. She knew Nell wished the two of them could share a hobby the way Charlotte and Aunt Linnea did.

Shrugging, Zibby stooped to peer into one of the castle's tower windows. Inside she could see a little gold throne with a blue velvet cushion. "It's okay," she offered grudgingly. But it wasn't special the way the old dollhouse was.

Nell sighed.

Zibby drifted back to the first house. She rubbed her hands over one of the velvety red cords placed to keep people from touching the displays.

*It's time for a change.*

The voice seemed to speak inside Zibby's head.

"Mom!" she cried, starting back toward them in confusion, when the bell rang again, a single peal followed by a frenzy of peals, as if the bell were being shaken vigorously by an unseen hand. She clutched the velvet rope dizzily, trying not to fall. For a moment she felt she couldn't breathe. The room seemed to dip and whirl around her, and she staggered. Then she felt a stinging in her hands, and looked down at her palms. Slowly they were reddening.

Something was happening. Something awful that she couldn't explain. . . . Zibby sucked air down into her lungs in a deep, desperate breath. She was trying to hold back a scream.

Then she heard a little disdainful laugh, and the ringing of the bell disappeared. The room stopped whirling. The sting in her palms receded.

"What an ugly dollhouse," said her cousin Charlotte, and gave that little laugh again. "Nobody would want a house like that. It's not even built to scale."

Zibby let out her breath slowly and blinked at the big, brown, boxy shape of the dollhouse in front of them. *What happened to me?* "Did you hear the bell?" she asked her cousin urgently.

"Bell?" Charlotte shook her head. "Nope."

Zibby looked at her hands. The palms still ached though the redness had faded. She could still hear the echo of the bells in her head. "Aunt Linnea, didn't you hear it?"

"Bell?" asked Aunt Linnea, walking up behind Charlotte. "I didn't hear a thing."

Zibby looked for her mother. "Mom?" Her voice rose anxiously. How could no one else have heard?

Nell shook her head and looked at her daughter curiously. "Do you feel okay, Zib?"

"Yeah, I guess so." But it wasn't true. She felt exhausted. And scared. And something else. She felt a strange yearning for something she'd never had before.

"Then," smiled Nell, "I guess it's on to Sportsmart!"

But Zibby put her hand on her mom's arm. "Mom, wait — look at this old dollhouse." Faintly, the ringing began again.

"It's the ugliest one I've ever seen," repeated Charlotte.

"It's pretty battered," Nell agreed. "Not much charm."

"A shack compared to the others." Aunt Linnea had walked over from the castle to inspect the dollhouse. "A shame, really. It might have been nice once. I'm surprised it's on display here at all. Who would want to buy it in that shape?"

Through her daze, her head still aching from the mysterious bell, Zibby reached for the tag attached by a string to the side of the ramshackle dollhouse. She turned it over to see the handwritten words:

Dollhouse, circa 1915. As is.
No refunds, no returns.
Only $85.76

Eighty-five dollars and seventy-six cents? She rubbed her hands together, then looked down at the palms. The redness was gone. Eighty-five dollars was every penny of her birthday money, every single cent of her Rollerblade savings. An old, filthy dollhouse. Ramshackle. A waste of good money. The last thing in the world she would ever want to own.

But Zibby knew one thing quite suddenly and with absolute certainty: She had to buy it. She could borrow the seventy-six extra cents from her mom if she had to. But, rooting, deep in the pocket of her shorts, she found three quarters and a penny she didn't know she had.

And no sooner had she pulled out the money, than an old woman with snow-white hair and sharp blue eyes approached her. She rubbed her wrinkled hands together. "Aha. You like my dollhouse, little one?"

Zibby nodded, holding out the coins.

Charlotte's voice filtered through the ringing. "Zibby? What in the world are you doing?"

It was a good question — no, a great question. What *was* she doing?

"You understand there are no refunds, my dear? The dollhouse is yours forever?"

Zibby nodded. She understood only that she had to have the house. It was, somehow, what she had been searching for.

The old woman rubbed her hands together again and an expression of relief flickered across her lined face.

"Good," she said.

*What in the world am I doing?* thought Zibby helplessly as she reached into her pocket for her wallet and took out all her Rollerblade money. But as much as a part of her wanted to snatch the money back, another part of her needed that old dollhouse in a way she had never needed anything before. When the old woman had pocketed the bills, the ringing in Zibby's head faded.

"But you don't even *like* dollhouses!" protested Charlotte.

"It's her decision," snapped the old woman. She scribbled on a slip of paper and thrust it at Zibby. "I need your signature right here," she said. "Your legal name. Saying you understand the nature of this sale." Zibby took the proffered pen and signed hastily:

*Isabel Thorne*

"Well," Aunt Linnea was saying, "Zibby's handy with tools. I'm sure the house can be fixed up." But she looked as surprised by the transaction as Charlotte.

"We can work on it together, if you like," said Nell. She gave Zibby a perplexed little smile. "You can do the structural repairs, and I'll help you with the furnishings. It's a real bargain, Zib. A marvelous investment."

Their voices breezed around her like a warm wind. Still feeling helplessly confused, Zibby turned and walked away from the dollhouse display area holding the scrap of paper the woman had given her. In a spidery hand the woman had written:

*Received for dollhouse: $85.76.*
*No refunds, no returns.*

It was Zibby's receipt for the house. She looked around for the old woman, but saw no sign of her.

No refunds, no returns.

Zibby was stuck. She had spent every cent of her birthday money on a dollhouse. She couldn't believe she had done it.

And for the life of her, she couldn't explain why.

# Chapter 3

## Primrose (1919)

Primrose Parson didn't *hate* her governess, not really. At least not enough to do something *truly* awful to her. But practical jokes were something else entirely. A good trick now and then made having to live with a governess like Miss Honeywell at bit more bearable.

Poor Primrose Parson, the housemaids whispered to each other as they passed the schoolroom door. Poor little Primrose, whose parents were as rich as kings, for all the good it did the child. Primrose herself never had more than a few pennies to spend at once — and only when Miss Honeywell could be bothered to take her out to the shops.

Primrose's parents spent most of the year away, traveling the world. When they were at home in their New York mansion, they were busy throwing or attending lavish parties. Their eldest daughter rarely saw them, rarely saw anyone but Miss Calliope Honeywell. Primrose hadn't seen much of them when Nanny Shanks was in charge, either, but then it hadn't mattered as much.

That was the time when Primrose had worn her hair in two thick, brown braids, always neatly tied with ribbons to match her dresses. Primrose's chubby body had glowed with health from playing out in Central Park with Nanny Shanks. Nanny always requested fresh bouquets of flowers for the nursery table. She was a gentle, kindly soul, good-humored and quick-witted. She was all Primrose had ever had in the way of a proper parent, and was all Primrose needed.

But then, last year on her eleventh birthday, Primrose's parents had decided the time had come for their oldest child to receive a more formal education than the old nanny could give her. She had been banished from the nursery, where dear Nanny Shanks remained to take care of the baby twins. Lucky little twins! But Primrose spent her days up in the schoolroom with Miss Honeywell.

The twins, Poppy and Basil, both fat and smiley, were a handful — two handfuls — and that meant Nanny Shanks needed the help of Bettie Sue, formerly one of the kitchen maids but now promoted to nursery maid. Now Nanny was no longer free to play with Primrose, or take her on walks to the park or to the zoo. Now that Primrose had moved out of the nursery and into the schoolroom, she never even saw her beloved Nanny Shanks or Bettie Sue anymore, nor the little twins.

Now she spent her days in the big, drafty schoolroom at the top of the house, and her nights in the little bedroom off the schoolroom. Miss Honeywell slept in an even smaller bedroom next to Primrose's. Primrose learned to braid her own hair, though the bows on the ends of the braids were never as jaunty anymore, and often came untied. She grew thinner from long hours of study and infrequent snacks. There was hardly any time for play because Miss Honeywell didn't believe in playing. Most of the toys had been left in the nursery. Worst of all, the dollhouse had been left for the little ones to play with. It was just a small wooden house with painted walls and a cheerful family of little stuffed mice living inside, but Primrose had pretended it was a fine mansion, furnished with beautiful furniture just like the things in her own house. She had spent hours making up games with the mouse family. In the schoolroom, when lessons with Miss Honeywell were over, Primrose longed to lose herself in the dollhouse. But Nanny had wanted to keep the house for the little ones. They liked the mouse family, too. And Primrose's parents wondered if she weren't getting too old for dolls, anyway.

Primrose knew she wasn't too old at all. She knew having a doll family like the little mice would help her forget about Miss Honeywell. She begged her father for a dollhouse of her own. And finally he had said that when he returned from his next trip abroad, he would see about getting one.

Primrose lay awake nights listening to Miss Honeywell snore. Nanny Shanks never snored. Nanny Shanks sang lullabies and told jokes and was always ready for a cuddle in the big rocking chair, even when Primrose was way too big to sit on anyone's lap anymore.

Miss Honeywell said she wanted to instill proper values in Primrose. She thought that Primrose was impudent and unladylike and needed to be taught manners. She believed that singing was frivolous and jokes were immoral. She didn't even have a lap, really. And who would want to sit on those unwelcoming, bony legs anyway?

It was the horrible, loud snoring that prompted the first practical joke Primrose played on the governess. Miss Honeywell's snoring sounded like the braying of a donkey. Primrose couldn't sleep. She tossed and turned in her narrow bed and then finally had an idea. She tiptoed out of bed and very quietly left her bedroom. The schoolroom was dark, but she crossed it carefully without lighting the lamp. She opened the door to the hall so slowly that it didn't even creak, and then she closed it behind her just as quietly. White nightdress billowing out around her, Primrose flew down three flights of stairs on silent, bare feet — down to the kitchen. The laundry was down yet another flight of steps, these of cold stone, in the big shadowy basement. Primrose crept along until she reached the laundry room. The vast metal sinks lined up against one wall and the wooden wringers seemed to watch as she sidled through the damp sheets to the bag hanging on the hook by the outside door. On warm sunny days the laundry maids hung the wet clothes out in the kitchen courtyard to dry. But on cold, gray winter days — the kind they'd been having now for what seemed to Primrose like forever — the laundry was hung up right here in the basement. It took much longer to dry. The bag on the hook contained clothespins. Primrose reached in and grabbed a handful.

Then she returned to her bedroom the way she had come, up the cold stone stairs to the quiet kitchen, along the back passage and through the butler's pantry to the dining room, out into the large front hallway, up the graceful, curving staircase to the third floor where the children slept. She hesitated a moment, debating whether to run down the hall to the nursery for a quick peek at the sleeping twins, and maybe a hug for Nanny Shanks. But the sleeping house was cold and her teeth were already chattering.

She turned and slipped back into the schoolroom. Over by the window was the wooden box that held her paints and colored pencils. She carried the box into her bedroom and knelt on the floor by the window, where cold moonlight illuminated a patch on the rug. She could see just well enough to draw the tiny figure of a donkey. She sketched it with gray pencil onto one side of the wooden clothespin, and, in bold red letters, printed *HEE HAW* on the other side.

Then she slipped into Miss Honeywell's bedroom. Miss Honeywell was a thin form on the bed, angular even under the warm blankets. Her mouth hung open and the snores rattled out from inside. Her mouse-brown hair, which by day she wore coiled tightly in a bun at the back of her neck, rested on the white pillow in two thin braids. Primrose regarded her with distaste.

*Nasty Old Honeywell! This will shut you up for a while.* Primrose slid the clothespin gently onto the governess's long nose, then pushed harder to wedge it firmly in place. Abruptly the snoring ceased. For a second all was quiet, then Miss Honeywell gasped and coughed.

Primrose stifled a giggle. Then she darted out of Miss Honeywell's bedroom and scurried back to her own. She leaped into her bed and drew the quilt up under her chin. Then she closed her eyes and pretended to be asleep. She tried to make herself breathe evenly as she heard the coughing from the other room continue. She counted slowly as she breathed — in, two three four; out, two three four — and heard the creak of the governess's bed. She continued counting as she heard the soft pad of the governess's slippered feet on the floor, and the creak of her own bedroom door as it opened.

She forced herself to keep breathing even when she sensed the governess standing by her bed.

"All right, young miss!"

Primrose opened her eyes as her covers were pulled off. "Oh, hello, Miss Honeywell," she exclaimed innocently. "Can it be morning so soon? I was having such a pleasant dream!"

"Get out of bed this instant, you naughty girl. I'll teach you about pleasant dreams!" The governess fastened her bony hand on Primrose's arm and dragged her out of bed. "You're coming with me, now." She led the girl out of the bedroom and back to her own room.

There she stood poor Primrose in the corner by the windows and wedged the clothespin onto Primrose's small nose. It was tighter than Primrose had thought, and pinched quite dreadfully.

She reached up to pull it off.

"Oh, no you don't, young miss," said the governess with spite in her voice. "You'll stand here for a full hour, wearing that on your nose. While wearing it, you shall be thinking about your unladylike deportment."

Primrose tried a smile, her most charming. "I was just trying to help you, Miss Honeywell. Your snores were so loud, I thought you might wake yourself up."

"Trying to help me, indeed!" Miss Honeywell slipped

back into her warm bed. "Now you just stand there and think about what deplorable manners you have."

Primrose glared at her governess, but didn't dare to reach up and remove the clothespin. *I'll take it off as soon as she goes to sleep,* she thought. But Miss Honeywell didn't go to sleep at all. Instead she lay there watching Primrose watching her. They watched each other for a full hour while Primrose's little nose ached and ached and finally grew numb. When the clock out on the landing chimed midnight, Miss Honeywell blew out her lamp and turned on her side.

"All right," she said. "You may go back to bed now, if you think you have learned your lesson."

Primrose snatched the clothespin off her nose.

"Have you learned your lesson, Primrose?"

"Yes," hissed Primrose. She muttered under her breath, "Yes, I have, you old sourpuss."

"Excuse me?" The governess's voice rose sharply.

"Yes, Miss Honeywell," said Primrose.

"That's *Sweet* Miss Honeywell to you, young miss."

"Yes, Sweet Miss Honeywell," repeated Primrose, longing to hurl the clothespin into the shadows where the governess lay, no doubt smiling smugly, in her bed.

But instead she left it on the windowsill and walked quietly out of the room, back to her own bed. She lay shivering under the quilt for a long time. Her nose throbbed.

Well, so much for *that* practical joke. But she would do better next time.

She started making plans. Salt in *Sweet* Miss Honeywell's sugar bowl — for a start. Cockroaches in her drinking glass. Dry, grainy, itchy washing powder sprinkled in her undergarments — the possibilities were endless.

Primrose rubbed her nose and smiled in the dark. Oh, yes, she would do better next time.

# Chapter 4

"It was such a treat to see your eyes light up when you first saw the dollhouse," Nell said as she helped Zibby lug it up the stairs to her bedroom.

"They didn't!" Zibby was appalled. Why couldn't she remember what had happened? Everything that had happened after they'd walked over to the dollhouse alcove at the convention hall was a blur. She had snapped out of her daze back into unwelcome clear focus when they were out in the parking lot, trying to load the big house into the back of Aunt Linnea's van. "Mom, I don't want this house!"

"Oh, honey." Nell smiled at Zibby. "I think your subconscious mind likes dollhouses after all. The house spoke to you."

"What do you mean?" Zibby asked in alarm.

"I mean it must have held some hidden charm for you. We'll fix it up and you can play with it." She shifted her end of the house as they headed down the hall to Zibby's room.

"But I don't like to play with dollhouses!" Zibby felt numb inside, numb from the shock of seeing her precious birthday money vanish on a dollhouse.

The house was heavy. And big. It would take up a lot of room. She didn't want it up in her bedroom at all. But Nell led the way over to the corner by the bookcase. They lowered the dollhouse carefully. It sat on the green carpet as if in a field. Zibby stepped back to look at it.

The three-story dollhouse stood as high as Zibby's waist, with a peaked roof. The brick chimney seemed solid enough, but some of the shingles were missing from the roof. There was a front porch with broken railings. The little windows had real glass in them, though the tiny panes of glass were clouded with the dirt of years. Aunt Linnea had given the house a cursory dusting before lifting it into the van just to get rid of the worst of the cobwebs, but plenty still remained.

Nell stooped to unfasten the catch and, with a creak, the front of the house swung open.

Despite herself, Zibby leaned forward. Inside the house were eight rooms, four upstairs and four downstairs. There was a single attic room and two little rooms inside the tower. She could see that the walls of all the rooms must once have been covered in delicate wallpaper, but they were now so old and dirty she could barely make out the patterns. Much of the paper hung in tattered strips. Most of the cobwebs were on the outside of the house, but some were inside as well, and thick layers of dust covered every surface. There was a staircase in the front hallway leading up to the bedrooms and then one more flight up to the attic. Bits of furniture lay tumbled across the wooden floors as if some previous owner had just tossed things around and slammed the door. The largest of the downstairs rooms was stuffed with some sort of patterned cloth. Zibby reached in her hand and tugged it out.

It was a large cloth bag, about the size of a pillow-case, printed with faded, yellow flowers. It had a dirty drawstring ribbon that might also once have been yel-low, pulled tightly closed. "What's this?" asked Zibby, and her mom held out a hand for the bag.

"Oh, Zib, you may have struck it lucky," murmured Nell as her fingers worked to untie the several knots in the ribbon. "If this is what I think it is . . ."

"What?"

Nell untied the knots and started to pull the bag open. But then she stopped and handed it over to Zibby. "You bought it, you get to open it."

Zibby felt a thrill of excitement. In books, kids were always finding hidden treasure. What if — what if there were jewels in this bag? Precious jewels stashed away by some long-ago family — and where better to hide them than in an old dollhouse where no thief would ever think to look? If the dollhouse held treasure, then her Rollerblade money would have been well-spent. Eagerly, she took the bag from her mother and spilled the contents out onto the green carpet of her bedroom floor.

Instead of a cascade of precious gems, a dozen tiny dolls dropped out. Zibby shook the bag, hoping for at least one jewel, and a few wads of folded cloth dropped out. Zibby gave the bag a last shake, then dropped it on top of the pile in disgust.

But Nell picked up the bag and looked down at the dolls. "What a find, Zib! This is so thrilling!"

"What?"

"Oh, Zibby, look at these — each one would have cost a bundle at the miniature show. And you've got, what, ten? Twelve? A whole little household of people to live in your house. And even some outfits for them — look at these." Nell was busily unfolding the wads of cloth. "Here's a dress for a little girl doll. Let's see if we can find one to wear it." Nell rummaged among the dolls and held up a little doll about four inches tall, with brown braids. "Here, this one looks sweet, honey! Let's dress her up."

"Oh, *Mom.*"

"And look at this one!" Nell held up a doll that was scaled larger than the others on the floor. It was about seven inches high and wore a long gray dress. Zibby thought its expression was unpleasant. Not a doll she would ever choose to play with even if she were the type to play with dolls.

Nell stood the dolls up inside the house and started sorting through the others. There were father and mother dolls, and servant dolls, and children dolls. Nell held each one up, excited about the fine quality of workmanship. But Zibby had had enough. She stood up and put her hands on her hips. "You can sit and play as long as you like," she told her mom. She stomped to her closet door and pulled out her helmet and her old, standard, boring skates. "But I'm outta here."

"Zibby, don't go far. Remember, we're going out for your birthday dinner —"

But Zibby didn't stay to listen. She raced down the stairs, fastening her helmet as she went, and ran out the front door. Then she sat on the steps to put on her skates. Stupid dollhouse. Stupid birthday dinner at a stupid restaurant with her stupid family. Why had Amy moved away? Why wasn't her dad here where he belonged? Everything was ruined.

She skated along the sidewalk under a canopy of green leaves from the oak trees that gave her street its name. Oaktree Lane was narrow and winding, and dead-ended at a little park where neighborhood parents brought their toddlers to play in the sandpit. Amy's house was the last house on the street by the park. Zibby skated with long, swinging swoops toward the park, determined not to look at her best friend's empty house.

Zibby couldn't imagine moving. She had lived in the house on Oaktree Lane her whole life. It was cozy and shabby, with peeling blue paint and a rickety front porch railing, and a front yard shaded with oak trees. It was the house her mom and Aunt Linnea had grown up in — though Aunt Linnea and her family now lived in a grand house across town. Aunt Linnea and Nell's parents, Zibby's grandparents, lived near the little train station now, in one of the new condominiums. Zibby loved her house, but it felt too big for just herself and her mother. Without her dad the rooms felt empty. Just as Oaktree Lane felt empty without Amy.

*Amy and Zibby — everything from A to Z,* they used to giggle to each other. But now there was an unfamiliar dark green car in the driveway of Amy's house. It hurt Zibby's eyes to look at it as she skated past. She entered the park and headed toward the playground. Then she heard a bell ring and her stomach clenched with fear.

But no, this bell was not in her head. She looked over the bushes separating the park from the street and saw that the bell ringer was a girl about her age who stood in Amy's driveway. She was tall and dark, and was waving a large handbell over her head. "Penny! Penny! It's dinnertime!" she called. And in another second a smaller girl shot off the slide and raced past Zibby on the path out of the park. "Coming!" the girl yelled back, and then she and the bell ringer disappeared inside Amy's house.

Zibby's heart leaped with excitement. Maybe Amy was back! Maybe her family had invited friends for dinner or something. Maybe they'd decided not to move after all. But then she saw the real estate sign still standing in the front yard, with a big, bold SOLD banner stretched across it. She noticed for the first time the big yellow moving van parked across the street from the house.

No, it had really happened. Amy was in Cleveland, and new people were moving in.

She skated slowly back down Oaktree Lane toward home, her heart heavy and sad.

# Chapter 5

Dinner at the Fat Lady was fun as long as Zibby kept herself from thinking about the dollhouse and the wasted eighty-five dollars, the postcard from Italy, the fact that Amy wasn't in her house anymore and two new girls were. Not thinking wasn't hard to do, really, because everyone was at last making a proper kind of fuss about her birthday. They sat at a large, round table in a corner of the restaurant, surrounded by potted fig trees, the soft light from old-fashioned brass lamps blanketing their corner in a warm glow. Glasses clinked around the room, and waiters spoke in muted voices. In the background, soft music played. Zibby didn't know what it was, but it had a lilting beat she thought of as Greek.

Everyone was trying to make Zibby feel better since Amy left. Even Charlotte had tried to be nice. She'd offered to throw a party in honor of Zibby's eleventh birthday, but Zibby hadn't wanted a party with Charlotte's friends who were as prim and bossy as Charlotte. She hadn't wanted a party without Amy. Then Nell suggested a dinner out at a restaurant instead of a party, and that idea suited Zibby just fine.

Now there were gifts to open while they waited for their food: a new box of watercolors from Nell, with a big block of paper to go along with it. A beautiful blue sweater from Aunt Linnea and Uncle David. A matching hairband covered in blue cloth from Charlotte. And Charlotte's brother, Zibby's fifteen-year-old cousin, Owen, gave her three paperback mysteries. The best present came from Grammy and Gramps, who waited eagerly while Zibby tore off the wrapping paper from the last gift.

"Ooh," said Charlotte. "I bet it's a jewelry box! Or a makeup kit!"

But it wasn't either, and for that Zibby was grateful. It was a toolbox from the hardware store, stocked full of real tools. A big smile broke over Zibby's face as she examined the hammer and screwdrivers, the hacksaw, the wrenches, pliers, and drills. Little plastic cases held screws, nails, nuts, and bolts.

But then she recalled how her dad had taught her to use tools and together they had made a birdhouse to hang out her bedroom window, a mailbox for their house, and a spice rack for her mom to hang up in the kitchen. When she wanted to move on to bigger projects, like a new bookcase for her bedroom, her dad had encouraged her to try it on her own. "You've got a touch of magic," he'd said. "Not everyone can work with wood."

Probably now he was teaching Sofia the magic.

Grammy was looking anxiously at Zibby. Zibby shook away the thoughts of her dad and smiled. "Thanks a zillion, Grammy and Gramps! This is *so* cool!"

Charlotte was shaking her head. "I don't *get* you, Zibby. You like the weirdest things!"

"Nothing wrong with a good set of tools," Gramps said. "Now you can help me mend your porch steps, Isabel. I was planning to do it over the weekend."

Gramps was the only one who always called Zibby by her real name. "Great!" she told him with a grin.

"And now you can use your tools to repair that wonderful old dollhouse," suggested Nell.

Zibby changed the subject quickly.

They ate pasta and salad, then Nell signaled to the waiter and he carried out a beautiful chocolate layer cake that Nell had made and arranged to have hidden away in the kitchen until the main course was over. The waiter gathered other waiters around him, and everyone sang "Happy Birthday" in rousing voices. Zibby blushed when the manager of the restaurant came out and handed her a single red rose, and everyone in the restaurant applauded.

Then one of the diners on the other side of the room detached himself from his party and sauntered across to their table. He had snapping black eyes beneath a fringe of thick, straight black hair. "Nell? Is it you?" He grinned at Zibby's mom.

"Ned!" she cried in delight, reaching up to touch his arm. "Look, everybody, it's Ned Shimizu! Remember him?"

It seemed all the adults did. Grammy and Gramps and Aunt Linnea shook the man's hand warmly.

Uncle David grinned. "Hello, Ned. It's been years since you made that home run that salvaged Carroway High's reputation. But I bet the kids there still talk about you."

The man laughed and said he doubted it. From the swell of chatter that ensued, Zibby figured out that this Ned Shimizu had been her mom's friend in high school. And he'd been a super baseball player for the school team. Uncle David and Aunt Linnea and Nell all seemed so happy to see him, but Zibby found herself a little annoyed. No one had even introduced her — or Charlotte or Owen for that matter. It was as if the people who hadn't already met this guy were invisible.

So she smiled up at him coolly and interrupted the flow of talk. "Hi, I'm Zibby and it's my birthday today. That's why everybody was singing. And that's why we came out to dinner in the first place."

Everyone laughed, except for Grammy, who gave Zibby a sharp glance. "I'm sorry, honey," apologized Nell. "Let me introduce you properly. Ned, this is my daughter Zibby — Isabel — who is eleven years old today. And this is my niece, Linnea and David's daughter, Charlotte." Charlotte actually held out her hand in a very proper grown-up way and shook Ned Shimizu's. "And my nephew, Owen," Nell continued. "He's going into tenth grade at our old school, so he'll be able to report back about whether you're still a legend there or not." Everyone at the table laughed comfortably.

"Hello, kids," Ned said. "Forgive me for interrupting your birthday celebration," he added, nodding at Zibby. "In fact, I've interrupted my own meal with my kids. But I just had to come over and say hello."

Zibby's mom asked him to sit down, but he shook his head. "No, I'll get back to my own table now. But stop by on your way out and I'll introduce you to Laura-Jane and Brady."

"Perhaps Charlotte and Zibby already know them from school," suggested Aunt Linnea.

"No, they wouldn't," said Ned. "My kids live with their mother over in Fennel. They go to school there, and stay with me in the summer and on some weekends." Fennel Grove was a town about three miles from Carroway. "I've been living and working in Columbus for years, but now I'm back in Carroway as the new features editor at the *Gazette*."

"That's wonderful," said Nell, and craned her neck to look over the heads of the other diners at Ned's children.

Then the waiter came to their table offering refills of coffee and tea, and Zibby asked for a cup of hot chocolate to end her birthday meal. Ned said goodbye and walked back to his own table. They stayed another twenty minutes while Nell, Aunt Linnea, and Uncle David told funny stories about their high school days. Owen was full of questions about the baseball team.

Soon Zibby was laughing so hard at some of the stories she spluttered her hot chocolate onto the tablecloth. Charlotte gave her a look and patted her lips primly with a napkin.

On their way out of the restaurant, they stopped briefly at Ned's table to meet his children. Brady was five years old. Laura-Jane was ten, and going into fifth grade, a year behind Zibby and Charlotte. Both Shimizu kids had the same thick, straight black hair and dark eyes. Brady grinned when they were introduced. But Laura-Jane ducked her head and flushed. "She's a little bit shy," commented Ned. "Say hi to my old friends, honey."

Laura-Jane bit her lip as she peered up at Zibby and her family. "Hi," she whispered, then ducked her head again so she wouldn't have to see them.

Charlotte rolled her eyes and nudged Zibby. *What*

*a baby!* her expression said. Zibby ignored her cousin, thinking to herself that it might be harder to be friends with bossy old Charlotte than with someone like Laura-Jane.

When she lay in bed that night, waiting for sleep, Zibby looked over at the birthday gifts piled on her night table and decided it had turned out to be a decent birthday, after all. Except for wasting her Rollerblade money. She tried to push the thought of the dollhouse out of her mind.

The dollhouse loomed in the shadows of her bedroom, an unfamiliar bulk by the bookcase. Zibby closed her eyes and turned over in bed. Her eyes popped open when she heard a sound from across the room. A scraping sound.

She sat up and stared into the shadows where the dollhouse stood. She remembered the flicker she thought she had seen in one of the upstairs windows while they were still at the miniature show. But there had been no sign of a mouse when Zibby opened up the house. Maybe there was a mouse after all? She told herself that's what it had to be — that, or just her imagination.

But no, there it was again. A tiny scraping sound, as if something were being dragged across the floor of the dollhouse. Then a clatter, and a tiny splashing sound.

She reached over to her bedside table and snapped

on the lamp. Warm light flooded the room and made weird sounds seem a silly dream. But she hadn't been asleep yet. So, slowly, Zibby slipped from her bed and crossed the room to the dollhouse. She would shut it and fasten the catch. That way if there were a mouse, it wouldn't be able to run around the bedroom at night. And in the morning she'd get her mom to help her set it free outside.

But what if it weren't a mouse?

Zibby knelt in front of the old, dirty house and peered inside. Nothing at all but the bag of dolls her mother had replaced in the downstairs room where they'd found it. But wait — a couple of the dolls had been left out. The doll in the gray dress stood propped in the upstairs hallway next to the little girl doll with the brown braids.

Zibby had to smile at the thought of how her mom must have been playing with the dolls after she'd gone out skating. And there was no sign of a mouse. She left the bag of dolls out on the rug, then closed the front of the house and fastened the catch. She climbed back into bed, and turned off the light. She lay there in the dark, listening hard, but she heard no more unusual sounds. She fell asleep wondering what to build with her new tools. She and Amy had started making a clubhouse in Amy's backyard, but now without Amy there was no reason for a club. Still, there must be something Zibby could build. Maybe she would repair the dollhouse after all. That way she could sell it for even more than eighty-five dollars and seventy-six cents. She could fix the porch and broken shingles, maybe even paint the whole house — and then get rid of it.

With these comforting thoughts she fell asleep.

# Chapter 6

In the morning Zibby awoke full of plans to begin renovations. She looked over at the dollhouse, bathed now in morning sunlight, and was surprised to see the doll in the gray dress sitting on the roof, leaning against the little brick chimney.

Her mom must really be into dolls if she was coming in to play with them before breakfast! Zibby jumped out of bed and threw on her favorite baggy blue shorts and a long, green T-shirt, then sauntered downstairs. Nell was sitting at the kitchen table, sipping coffee and reading the newspaper. She looked up with a smile when Zibby came in.

"Good morning, sweetheart."

"Morning."

"Here, finish off this cereal, would you? Then we can add the box to the recycling bin before it gets picked up today." Nell handed Zibby the box of bran flakes.

Obligingly, Zibby shook the last of it into her bowl. Then she poured herself a glass of milk, splashed some of it onto the cereal, and sat down with her mom. "I didn't even hear you come in," she said.

Nell looked up from the paper. "In where?"

"Into my bedroom this morning. Or in the middle of the night. When you were playing with the dollhouse."

"I didn't come into your room, honey. What makes you think so?" Nell laid down the paper and looked across the table with a puzzled expression.

Zibby was silent for a long moment, remembering the noises she'd heard in the night. "The dolls," she said finally. "I put them into the bag last night and left it on the floor, but now the bag is open and one of the dolls is sitting on the roof."

"Well, then you must have been playing with them in your sleep," teased Nell. "I haven't been in your room at all."

Zibby picked at her cereal. Why would her mom lie? "I wasn't playing with them."

Nell laughed. "Then I guess the doll just walked right out by itself." She finished her orange juice and folded the newspaper. "I've got to leave in ten minutes," she said. "But I'll try to be home for lunch. There's a lot to do this week for the big Isaac wedding."

Zibby's mom owned her own catering business. She prepared feasts for many important festivities that took place in Carroway and Fennel Grove. Zibby sometimes worked with her on the weekends. It was fun to cook together in their large kitchen, specially equipped with two stoves, two refrigerators, and, in the pantry, an extra large freezer. It was fun, too, to help serve food at fancy parties or to be in charge of placing the last delicate fringes of cilantro on platters of delicious appetizers.

"In fact," Nell went on, "maybe I should arrange for you to stay with Linnea today while I'm working. I may be gone until dinnertime."

"I can stay alone, Mom." Zibby glowered at her mom. "After all, I'm eleven now." *Really,* she fumed to herself. First her mom went sneaking around in the night, playing with dolls, and now she was treating Zibby like a child.

"I think you'd have more fun playing with Charlotte, honey. I don't like to think of you here alone all day, moping around without Amy." Nell cleared her coffee mug to the sink and left the kitchen. She returned a moment later carrying her car keys.

Her mother refused to understand that Zibby never had fun playing with Charlotte anymore.

"Listen, Mom," pleaded Zibby. "I'll be *fine.* I won't mope at all. I want to work on fixing up the dollhouse with my new tools." She didn't mention that she was going to sell the house as soon as it was repaired.

"Well . . ." Nell dropped a kiss on top of Zibby's

gold-red hair and went to the back door. "I'll call if I can't come home for lunch, and if I can't, I want you to go over to Aunt Linnea's. She'll feed you, at least."

As if Zibby weren't capable of making a sandwich! "Okay, Mom," Zibby said in a tight voice. There was no point arguing. But at least she wasn't stuck with having to hang out with Charlotte all day.

After Nell left, Zibby finished her cereal and then went back upstairs to her room. Just inside the bedroom door she stopped with a gasp. The dolls she had left on the floor in front of the house were no longer there. They were back inside the dollhouse.

Quickly she crossed the room, her hand pressed to her mouth. Then, after a second, her fear was replaced by anger. Her mom must have run up and moved the dolls when she went out of the room to get her car keys.

Teasing wasn't Nell's usual style, and Zibby didn't like it. If her mom liked playing with dolls so much, Zibby decided, then her mom could just keep the dollhouse in her *own* bedroom.

Lips pressed tightly together, Zibby tossed the dolls into the sack, then shoved the sack into the house. She shut the front of the house and latched it. Then she wrapped her arms around the structure and tried to lift it. Too heavy. She tried to push it, but it caught in the rug and wouldn't budge. She hesitated, then had the idea to work her quilt underneath the house. She could pull it along on top of the quilt.

It worked like a perfect sled. The dollhouse slid along silently behind her on the quilt as Zibby pulled it down the hall to her mom's bedroom. Inside, she dragged it off the quilt and left it in the corner by Nell's dresser. *There you go. Play with the dolls all you like, Mom!*

As she left the room carrying her quilt, she thought for a second she heard the ringing of a bell. She tried to pretend she didn't hear it. But the stinging in her palms was harder to ignore. She clutched the folds of the soft quilt tightly and continued down the hall to her room.

By the time she'd settled the quilt back at the foot of her bed, her hands felt fine again. Zibby told herself she had just imagined the stinging. She decided to skate in the park until lunchtime.

Off she went, along Oaktree Lane. She skated along past all the houses so similar in style to her own, but painted a rainbow of colors. When she reached the end of the street, where the park entrance lay between two tall oak trees, she pivoted, and skated to the driveway of Amy's yellow house. She skated back and forth in front of the yellow house, but didn't see any sign of the new girls. The moving van was gone, too.

Then she heard banging from the backyard. For a second she could almost believe it was Amy back there, working on their clubhouse. Amy was good with tools, too, and had once even used a power saw by herself.

But Zibby knew it couldn't be Amy. What if someone were wrecking the clubhouse they had started building?

Zibby skated slowly down the driveway to the backyard. The girl named Penny was kneeling in the yard beside the pile of boards Amy's dad had given them for their clubhouse. The girl was trying to hammer two of the boards together with wide, awkward swings of her arm. She was missing the nail nearly every time and banging instead on the wood, or on the driveway. If she didn't watch out, she'd be banging her hand next.

It hurt Zibby to see the boards intended for the clubhouse being messed with, but Amy's parents had refused to take them along to Cleveland. Amy had said Zibby could have them, but without Amy, what was the point of having a clubhouse anyway?

"Hello, Penny," Zibby said.

The girl turned, her dark eyes wide and startled. She looked about Zibby's age, maybe a little younger. "Who are *you*? And how come you know my name?"

"I heard someone calling you when you were playing in the park."

"Oh." The girl tilted her head and her dozens of tiny braids moved, the beads at the ends clicking prettily. "That must have been Jude, ringing me home for dinner."

Zibby looked at the yellow house. "Is your sister inside?"

"Nope. She's not my sister — and she's not home. She's out with my mom buying stuff. It's a lot of trouble to move."

"Where did you move here from?"

"Pennsylvania. And I wish we hadn't come."

"Me too," said Zibby. Then, seeing the hurt expression flash across Penny's face, she tried to explain. "I mean, I wish my best friend hadn't moved away to Cleveland. This is her house. I mean, it *was*."

"Oh. Too bad," said Penny. She looked as if she meant it, and Zibby felt friendlier. "So, what's your name?"

"Zibby Thorne." She wanted to ask more about the other girl, Jude, but Penny didn't give her the chance.

"Zibby's a funny name."

"Well, so's Penny." Zibby was used to having people comment on her unusual nickname. "My real name is Isabel. I'm eleven. How old are you?"

Penny swung her hammer again and tried to hit the nail in the plank she was holding. "I'm ten," she said. "And my real name is Penelope, but no one calls me that, thank goodness. I *hate* the name Penelope. Do you hate Isabel?"

"No, I like it. It's an old family name. But when I was little, my cousin — she's a couple months older than me and learned to talk first — started calling me Zibby, and the name stuck." Giving her a cool nickname was about the only nice thing Charlotte had ever done for her, thought Zibby grimly. Then she looked at Penny and gestured toward the boards. "Anyway, what are you doing with these?"

Penny scowled. "I'm trying to build a dollhouse. But it isn't working."

*Dollhouses, again!* Zibby shook her head. "Well, that's because these boards are too big for a dollhouse. And too thick." She hesitated, picturing the clubhouse as she and Amy had planned.

"There are some smaller pieces from some wooden crates we used for moving," said Penny. "Would they work?"

Zibby inspected the crates. "Maybe." She hesitated, then added, "I'm pretty good with tools. I could help you, if you want."

"Hey, that would be great!" Penny started piling the heavy boards back into a pile. "We can use these for something else sometime."

Penny showed Zibby the sketch of the dollhouse she wanted. It looked complicated, fancy. "You're good at drawing," Zibby said, "but I don't think you can make this kind of house out of crates. You need better wood. This is too rough." She thought of the dollhouse back at her own house, and smiled. "Wait, Penny. Would you like to buy a house instead of build it? I've got a really nice one you can buy. It needs some repairs, but it costs only eighty-five dollars."

"Eighty-five dollars seems like a lot. I don't have

that much money. I only have about ten dollars, and I was saving up for dollhouse furniture."

Now that she had a potential buyer for her dollhouse, Zibby didn't want to lose her. "Well, maybe your mom or dad will help you buy it. Or maybe I can lower the price, although that is supposed to be a really good price because the house is sort of a fixer-upper. I've seen dollhouses that cost *thousands* of dollars."

Penny looked unconvinced. She picked up her sketch and looked down at the crates.

"Do you want to come see it, at least?" pressed Zibby.

"Well, okay. Let me go tell my mom."

Penny darted into the back door of Amy's yellow house and then in a moment was back again. "It's okay," she said. "But I need to be home for lunch in a half hour."

Zibby skated along slowly next to Penny, who was chattering a mile a minute about the dollhouse furniture she'd seen at a store in Pennsylvania. "It was really neat," she giggled. "Little table and chairs with hearts painted on them. It looked like something from a fairy tale, or from the Three Bears. Maybe I'll get a bear family for my dollhouse. But right now I have trolls. You know, with the long hair and squashed faces. What kinds of dolls live in your dollhouse?"

"Oh, I don't know," Zibby replied carelessly. "Old-fashioned ones." Up ahead a girl who looked from the back like Charlotte turned the corner on her bike and disappeared. Zibby waved to Mr. Simms, their across-the-street neighbor. Then she turned into her own driveway and spun around neatly to sit on the porch steps to unbuckle her skates.

Skates and helmet in hand, she led Penny into her house. She dumped her skates and helmet into the closet by the door and then climbed the stairs to her mom's room. "I think you'll really like this house," she was saying as she walked across the room. "It's got loads of space for a bear family — " She broke off in confusion. The dollhouse was no longer where she'd left it by her mom's dresser.

Perplexed, she walked out of the room. "Mom? Are you home?" But how could Nell be home when the car wasn't in the driveway?

Zibby wheeled around and pushed past Penny to go down the hall to her own bedroom. She stopped at her doorway when she heard the bell in her head, ringing as if from a great distance.

"What is it?" asked Penny, behind her. "Is something wrong?"

The palms of Zibby's hands started stinging. Holding her breath, she peered into her bedroom — and gasped.

The dollhouse was back.

# Chapter 7

Slowly Zibby crossed the room to stand in front of it. The house was still latched, but the sack of dolls was lying open on the floor. One of the dolls lay on the floor of the front porch. It was the girl doll with the brown braids, wearing the old-fashioned yellow dress that Nell had dressed her in the day before.

Zibby stared at the doll. It stared back blankly. Who had brought the house back into the bedroom? Who had played with the dolls?

It *had* to be her mom. But her mom wasn't home.

Zibby looked around wildly, as if expecting to see Nell hiding somewhere. But instead she noticed something on top of her pillow. She walked over to the bed and frowned down at the doll perched there. It was the larger doll, the one with the unpleasant expression, wearing the long, gray dress. Her stern painted mouth seemed to be turned down even further than before, and her painted eyes glared up at Zibby.

"Well, don't look at *me,*" muttered Zibby, reaching for the doll with distaste. "*I* didn't put you here." She tossed the doll across the floor by the dollhouse, not caring in the least whether she cracked the little porcelain head or hands.

She stood by her bed, debating whether to say anything about what was going on to Penny or not. But what could she say? What *was* going on? It didn't make sense.

While she lingered, Penny turned to inspect the dollhouse. "This is beautiful!" she exclaimed. "I'd *love* to buy it. I'll definitely ask my mom to lend me some money. Maybe it could be a birthday present — even though my birthday is still months away."

Zibby jumped when the doorbell pealed downstairs. She left Penny entranced by the dollhouse and ran from the bedroom, down the stairs to the front door. She could see Charlotte standing outside the screen door.

"You're supposed to come over to my house for lunch," Charlotte announced. "My mom says your mom called her. So I've come to get you. We can go on our bikes."

"You didn't need to come get me. I'm perfectly capable of riding over on my own." Zibby's heart was still thumping hard from her earlier fright. She didn't actually feel capable of walking back up the stairs, much less riding her bike across town.

"My mom called, but you weren't home. And I was riding my bike around anyway, so I thought I'd just stop by." Charlotte reached back and lifted her curls off her shoulders. "It's hot out here," she complained. "Hurry up and let's go."

Zibby remembered seeing Charlotte ride by when she and Penny were on their way home. Had Charlotte already been over here to the house? Had she let herself in with the key Aunt Linnea kept for emergencies? Had Charlotte been the one who moved the dollhouse?

Zibby sighed with a sudden enormous relief. Of course it had been Charlotte. That explained everything. "It's not nice to come in and play with other people's things without asking," she told her cousin sternly. "Even if we *are* related."

Charlotte looked at her with raised eyebrows. "What are you talking about?" Of course, Charlotte always managed to sound innocent.

"You know perfectly well," Zibby snapped back. "And so you can just wait. I've got a friend over."

"What friend?" laughed Charlotte. "Your only friend in the world has moved away. You don't have a friend left."

Just then Penny appeared at the top of the stairs. "Oh, there you are," she said to Zibby.

"This is my cousin, Charlotte Wheeler," said Zibby grudgingly. "And this is Penny."

"Penny Jefferson," Penny added shyly. "We just moved here. From Pennsylvania."

"Penny?" said Charlotte with a sniff. "Got a brother named Dime?" She giggled, pleased at her own wit.

Penny sighed. Zibby bet she'd heard the joke before. "No, his name is Malcolm."

"I have to go to Charlotte's for lunch," Zibby told Penny. "But I'll be back later and you can come over again."

The three girls stepped out onto the porch and Zibby locked the door behind them. Charlotte went to her bike, which was parked in the driveway. Zibby headed for the garage in back to get hers. As Penny started walking home, Zibby turned and called to her. "Be sure to ask your mom about the dollhouse!"

"I will!" Penny called back, and waved.

Charlotte frowned when Zibby joined her with her bike. "What was that about the dollhouse?"

"I'm selling it. Penny wants to buy it."

"Zibby! You can't sell it! You just bought it."

"It's mine, and I can sell it if I want to."

Charlotte mounted her bike and set off ahead of Zibby. "I think you should keep it."

"Why?" Zibby called ahead to her cousin as they rode down Oaktree Lane. "So you can sneak in and mess with it when I'm not home? Why don't you just buy it from me? That would save you the trouble of coming over."

Charlotte braked and stared back at her. "What are you talking about?"

Zibby felt a stab of misgiving. If it hadn't been Nell playing with the house in the night, and it hadn't been Charlotte sneaking in and moving the house back to Zibby's room, then what on earth was going on? She shook her head. "I think you know very well," she told Charlotte.

"I know you're crazy, Zibby Thorne. That's what I know." Charlotte set off again, her back straight, her blonde curls swishing indignantly on her shoulders as she rode.

Zibby followed slowly behind. She tried to ignore the niggling worry that maybe her cousin was right.

# Chapter 8

Zibby and Charlotte ate egg salad sandwiches in Charlotte's garden. This wasn't unusual; it was where they often ate when Zibby stayed for lunch with her cousin. But in the past they had sat on the grass, gobbled sandwiches from plastic picnic plates, then swung on the rope swing hanging from the elm tree. Now they sat on ornate wrought-iron chairs at a table covered with a lace cloth. Their sandwiches were cut into dainty triangles and arranged on china plates. They drank juice from thin china teacups. The rope swing had been taken down a couple months ago, when Charlotte decided she was too grown-up for such childish things. Zibby missed it.

Charlotte had decided she was a lady last January, at her eleventh birthday party, and Zibby liked her even less since then. Charlotte had always been bossy, but in January she became prim and proper as well as bossy. All her party guests had been told to dress up in their fanciest clothes and Aunt Linnea had served the party food as if they were attending an elegant afternoon tea. Zibby had fun at the party, though was glad to get out of her little-worn dressy clothes afterward. But Charlotte changed after the party. She dressed up in the newest styles, talked about clothes a lot, wanted to go to the mall in Fennel Grove all the time, and even started getting gooey over boys. She packed away all of her toys — except the dollhouse, which didn't count as a toy, she explained, because it was her hobby, just as it was her mother's hobby.

Zibby drained her juice and set the teacup back onto its saucer. She pushed back her wrought-iron chair and stood up. "I'm going now," she said, interrupting Charlotte, who had been chattering on about a cute guy who was a friend of Owen's.

"What?" Charlotte stopped in mid-sentence. "But my mom said you were going to be here for the afternoon. Lindsay and Jennifer are coming over and we're going to try out some makeup our moms got us. I want you to stay so we can fix you up. With a little mascara and blush and eyeshadow, you could look much better, Zibby. Now that you're eleven, don't you think it's time to grow up a little?"

Zibby just stared at her. The last thing she wanted was to smear makeup on her face. "No way," she said. "I'm going to see that new girl, Penny."

Charlotte arched her brows. "That little girl in the overalls? She looked about six."

"She's ten," Zibby retorted. "You were ten not very long ago yourself."

Charlotte sighed, shaking her head as if Zibby were a grave disappointment to her. "Well, I guess you'll grow up sometime," she said primly. "People mature at different ages. I guess you're just not ready."

Zibby strode off toward the house without another word. She would have liked to jump on her bike and ride straight home, but first she knew she had to tell Aunt Linnea she was leaving.

Aunt Linnea looked surprised. "I thought you were going to stay and play with Charlotte," she said. Zibby explained that Charlotte's friends were coming over and that she was going to visit the new people who had moved into Amy's house. Aunt Linnea nodded. "Well, I suppose that will be fine. I'll just bring Charlotte over when Uncle David and I leave tonight. I've arranged with your mom for her to spend the night with you two since we'll be out late and Owen will be out, too." Usually when Aunt Linnea and Uncle David were out late, Charlotte stayed home with Owen. Zibby knew her cousin would be furious not to be allowed to stay home alone. She smiled inwardly. So much for being all grown-up. *Too bad for you, Char!*

"Fine. See you later then," was all Zibby said. "Thanks for lunch, Aunt Linnea." And then she was off on her bike, hurrying back across town to Oaktree Lane.

She was fuming as she rode along, thinking of Charlotte and her friends talking about her as they primped and preened in front of the mirrors, plastering their faces with makeup. Saying how immature poor Zibby was.

She rode through the park and stopped at Amy's house — that is, Penny's house — but no one came to the door when she rang the bell. She rode on down the street to her own house and let herself in the front door with her key. The house was as humid outside as inside, and Zibby wished her house had central air-conditioning the way Charlotte's house did. Only the bedrooms were air-conditioned in Zibby's house.

She poured herself a glass of peach juice and took it upstairs to her room. She closed the bedroom door and turned on the air-conditioning, wondering how long before Penny came home from wherever she had gone. She wondered whether Penny's mom would let her buy the dollhouse.

Zibby knelt on the floor in front of the dollhouse. She picked up the mother doll and looked at it for a moment. Then she gently set it in a chair at the kitchen table. Then she picked up the red-haired doll in the maid's dress and set it near the mother doll in the kitchen. There. That was just the way she and her mom sat together for meals. Zibby studied the dolls for a moment, then picked out a blonde doll from the pillowcase. This would be the Charlotte doll, coming over for dinner because her parents weren't home.

"'Okay, Zibby,'" she made the mother doll say. "'Now that dinner is over, it's time for us to put little Charlotte to bed.'"

"'You can't put me to bed,'" the Charlotte doll answered haughtily. "'I am not a baby.'"

"'Oh, yes, you are,'" said the Zibby doll. Zibby exchanged the Charlotte doll for a tiny baby doll from the pillowcase pile. It was wrapped in a scrap of faded green cloth. "'See? A little baby who needs to go straight to bed.'" She made the Zibby doll carry the baby up the dollhouse stairs. "'And bad little babies who go sneaking into other people's houses and messing with their things have to go straight to bed.'" She walked the dolls into the little dollhouse bathroom. "'But first, we have to wash off all that eye shadow. Babies look stupid wearing eye shadow.'"

Downstairs the front doorbell jangled. The sound was dim, muffled by the closed door and the hum of the air conditioner, but Zibby heard it with relief. It was probably Penny. She laid the red-haired doll on the dollhouse floor, and dropped the baby into the bathtub. Then she ran downstairs.

Through the screen door she saw Penny standing out on the porch. The taller girl was with her. That must be Jude.

*They've got to be sisters,* thought Zibby, taking in the girls' identical braids and beads, their heart-shaped faces, warm brown eyes and skin, and matching smiles.

"Hi," she said, opening the door wide. "Come on in."

"Hi," Jude said. "Penny told me about you."

"Penny says you're not her sister," Zibby told her, "but that's hard to believe. Are you cousins? My cousin Charlotte and I don't look anything alike, though. She's tall and blonde." *And stuck-up as anything.* "Let's go upstairs to my room. The air-conditioning is on up there."

"We're not sisters — and we're not cousins, either," Penny said with a mischievous grin as they started up the stairs. "Guess again."

"Oh, Penny, don't always make it into such a big deal." Jude sounded embarrassed. "She's my aunt, that's all."

"Your *aunt?*" Zibby asked in astonishment.

"That's right," said Jude firmly. "My dad is Penny's big brother. My parents are out of the country this year, working at a hospital in Kenya. They're both doctors. So I'm living with my grandparents." She poked Penny. "And my Aunt Penelope."

Penny poked her back. "If you call me that again, I'll shave your head while you sleep."

Zibby was trying to figure it out. "You mean," she said to Penny, "your mom and dad are Jude's *grandparents?*"

"Yup," said Penny. "And she calls them Nana and Noddy. Isn't that weird?"

"You're what's weird around here," Jude told her. "Whoever heard of a ten-year-old aunt?"

"If you're mean to me," Penny warned her, "I'll —"

"I know, I know," sighed Jude. "You'll shave my head while I sleep."

Then the two of them giggled, and Zibby realized they were friends as well as antagonists.

"But if you shave my head," continued Jude, "then I'll be totally bald and funny-looking and still calling you *Aunt Penelope* every day of your life. So watch yourself."

The three girls went down the hall to Zibby's bedroom. Penny ran right over to the dollhouse. "Look, Jude. This is the dollhouse I told you about."

"Only eighty-five bucks," said Zibby. "Dolls included." She wouldn't make Penny pay the additional seventy-six cents. That had been a weird price to ask, anyway.

"Really? That's a lot of money." Jude shook her head.

"It is — but you should see how much other dollhouses cost. Two or three or four times this much. Some of the antique ones cost thousands of dollars. And this dollhouse is an antique."

"But I don't have eighty-five bucks," said Penny mournfully. "And Mom says she has to think about it."

"She'll give in," predicted Jude. "Tell them it can be a moving-in present for you." She rolled her eyes at Zibby. "Penny is spoiled rotten. I guess it's not totally her fault, but she gets away with murder. It's because my nana had tried for years and years to have another child after my dad was born, and finally gave up. Then, when my dad was all grown-up and married to my mom, and I was a brand-new baby, Nana got pregnant with Penny."

"She calls me her Miracle Dream Baby," said Penny importantly.

Jude made gagging sounds.

While Penny examined the dollhouse, Jude and Zibby sat on her bed. It was easy to talk to Jude — not like talking to Amy, of course, who had known her forever, but not like talking to Charlotte, either, where there seemed to be no meeting ground anymore. Zibby and Jude found they had a lot in common. They were both eleven. They were both going into sixth grade when school started. They both had to deal with troublesome people in their families — Charlotte, in Zibby's case; Penny, in Jude's — though Zibby had to admit to Jude that she liked Penny and didn't see anything troublesome about her. "Oh, you will," prophesied Jude. But then she smiled.

They were both interested in building things: Zibby wanted to become a carpenter, and Jude wanted to be an architect. She went over to inspect the dollhouse. "Somebody did a fantastic job building this old house," Jude said. "Why do you want to sell it?"

Zibby started to explain how she hadn't meant to buy the house, but then she realized how odd her story would sound. She broke off and shook her head. "I don't play with dolls much," she said simply. "I want Rollerblades instead."

"Hey, I love to Rollerblade. Penny's good, too. Let's go this afternoon!"

Zibby nodded, and the long days of summer ahead of her suddenly didn't seem so empty.

"Hey, look at the ugly mug on this one," Penny called out, holding up the doll in the gray dress. "She's not very nice, is she? I don't think she really belongs here with the other dolls."

"I don't like her either," said Zibby.

Penny tossed the grim-faced doll aside and reached for the sack of dolls. She started arranging them on the couches and chairs in the dollhouse living room. "How come the house is so dirty, Zibby?" she asked. "It would be really pretty if the wallpaper were cleaned up and stuff."

"It came that way," Zibby explained. "Probably it was up in somebody's storage room for a zillion years. Who knows?"

"Why is this baby doll on her head in the tub?"

"Leave her there," said Zibby firmly. "That's where she belongs."

Zibby, Jude, and Penny spent the rest of the afternoon skating in the park. Jude even let Zibby try out her Rollerblades. Zibby's heart felt lighter than it had in three weeks — ever since she'd learned that Amy was going to move. Of course the new girls could never replace Amy — no one could. But they were fun to be with, and Zibby was able to put the dollhouse out of her mind.

Nonetheless, when Zibby heard the clang of a bell, she froze for a second. Would the stinging palms come next? She held her breath, waiting, then relaxed when she realized the bell was a dinner bell.

"That's Nana," said Jude. "Suppertime. I've got to set the table." She started skating with long, graceful strides. "Come on, Penny."

Zibby skated with them, waving good-bye at the yellow house. Then she went home, where her own mom was in the kitchen getting dinner ready. They were having Zibby's favorite — baked macaroni and cheese with a big salad and fresh green beans from Gramps' garden. Zibby hummed as she washed the lettuce leaves, tore them into bite-size pieces, and whirred them dry in the salad spinner. She felt happy, and talked excitedly, telling Nell all about Jude and Penny.

The screen door banged. "Nell?" called Aunt Linnea. "Charlotte's here."

"We're in the kitchen," called Nell in return.

Aunt Linnea walked into the kitchen, dressed in an elegant backless black sundress. "David's waiting in the car," she said. "We're a little late. We've got to rush or we won't make it before the boat leaves. Now, Char," she said to Charlotte, who was standing right behind her, "you be a good girl and have fun. We'll see you later."

Charlotte entered the kitchen sulkily. "Bye-bye, Mama," she said in a fake little-baby voice.

Aunt Linnea rolled her eyes, then waved and was gone. Nell came over and gave Charlotte a kiss. "How are you, honey? Ready for dinner?"

Charlotte turned her face away from Nell's kiss. She slumped down in a chair at the kitchen table, her face sullen. "I just hate the way she treats me like a baby," she fumed. "There's no reason why I shouldn't be able to stay home alone! It's only a few hours."

"Well," said Nell cheerfully. "We're glad to have you spend the night with us. Right, Zib?" When Zibby didn't answer immediately, Nell frowned at her. She put her hand on Charlotte's shoulder. "And, really, your mom told me it would be well after midnight before they get home. Your dad's office party is known for lasting way into the wee hours. And this one is special, or so he told me. His new client is holding the party on one of those big riverboats!"

"I don't care," muttered Charlotte. "It isn't fair. Jennifer and Lindsay are eleven and they can stay home alone. They can also stay out till midnight, if they want. And go on dates."

"Dates?" laughed Nell. "That's silly. They aren't even in junior high yet!" She slid a plate of macaroni and salad in front of Charlotte. Charlotte pushed it away, burst into tears, and ran out of the room.

Nell and Zibby looked at each other. "Uh-oh, I can see the teenage years are approaching," said Nell ruefully. "I hope Linnea's got a strong stomach."

"What does that mean?" asked Zibby, perplexed and embarrassed by her cousin's behavior. Then they heard a thump overhead and a cry, and both of them rushed for the stairs.

The bathroom door was closed, but a thin trickle of red seeping under the door alerted them to look inside. There they discovered Charlotte, sprawled on the floor, her forehead streaming blood from where she'd fallen and struck it on the side of the tub.

# Chapter 9

"Charlotte, Charlotte, oh, no!" cried Nell.

Zibby was holding her breath, but let it out in a *whoosh* when, after a second, Charlotte opened her eyes. She stared up at them, dazed.

"I — I don't know what happened," sobbed Charlotte, no longer a sullen young lady but a scared little girl. She clung to Nell's arm.

"No, don't move, darling," cautioned Nell as Charlotte tried to sit up. "You were unconscious for a moment, and you may have a concussion."

Zibby felt relief at her mom's professional tone. Nell would know what to do to help Charlotte. All Zibby's earlier annoyance at her cousin evaporated at the sight of Charlotte lying bloody on the floor. The gash was wide and deep. It made Zibby feel sick. And Charlotte could only be feeling worse.

"I was just standing at the sink, looking in the mirror, and then I thought I saw one of you coming into the room behind me," Charlotte was explaining. "But it couldn't have been, because neither of you is wearing gray — anyway, I don't know, I slipped somehow." She put a hand tentatively to her head, moaned when she saw the blood. "Oh, Aunt Nell!"

Swiftly, Nell pressed a clean towel to the gash, then helped her niece sit up. "You're going to need stitches, I'm afraid. Can you stand up, sweetheart? We need to get you to the hospital on the double."

"Poor Char," sighed Zibby. She went to the sink, carefully stepping over the blood on the floor, and filled a cup with cold water. "Here, can you drink this?"

Charlotte reached out a hand, then dropped it again. "No — I can't. Oh, Aunt Nell, I'm so dizzy . . ."

Nell frowned. "Straight out to the car, honey. I'll help you walk."

"Shouldn't Charlotte go in an ambulance?" worried Zibby. On TV she'd seen people with lesser injuries than Charlotte's whizzing away in ambulances, lights flashing. She followed her mom and cousin down the hall, then down the stairs, one slow step at a time. She felt helpless and miserable. She remembered the last time she'd felt this lurching sickness in her belly. It had been three years ago when her father had cut off the tip of his big toe with the lawn mower. She hated when anyone in her family was sick or hurt.

Nell settled Charlotte in the car and gave her another clean towel to press against the gash on her head. Nell looked worried when she saw that the bleeding had not stopped. "Zibby, this might take a while. You'd better call Grammy. She or Gramps can come get you and take you home so you won't be here alone."

"I'm old enough. I can just stay here." She felt like an echo of Charlotte.

"All right." Clearly Nell was in no mood to debate the issue just now. "Lock the doors — and if you get lonely, give them a call. I'll call you if we're going to be gone past bedtime."

They drove off, Charlotte silent and drooping in the front seat next to Nell. Zibby waved until the car turned the corner, even though she knew neither of them was watching. Then she climbed the steps of the porch and sat down in the old rocking chair.

The summer evening was still. The crickets and fireflies were just starting to come out, and the people who had been mowing their lawns or watering their gardens had gone inside. Probably most families were eating dinner. Zibby stood up and walked around restlessly, then went inside again. She left the front door open, locking the screen. She was drawn into the kitchen by the smell of macaroni and cheese.

Nell had left the casserole cooling on the counter by the microwave. Zibby spooned a large portion into a bowl, ignored the beans and salad, and carried the bowl up to her bedroom. Something drew her over to the dollhouse. She knelt on the floor in front of it and heard the bell ring, just once, quite softly. She knew it couldn't be the Jeffersons' dinner bell. It was higher in tone, more strident; it was the bell inside her head.

She looked into the dollhouse and her heart thudded with guilty recognition when she saw the baby doll in the scrap of green fabric — the Charlotte doll. It was lying where she'd dropped it this afternoon — right in the little bathtub, its little forehead pressed hard against the cold porcelain.

In her mom's bedroom, the telephone rang. Zibby jumped up and ran to answer. It was Penny, screeching with excitement because her mother had said she could buy Zibby's dollhouse.

"That's great," said Zibby, a giddy sense of relief flooding through her at Penny's news. *Idiot,* she told herself. *It's only a dollhouse.*

"But you have to clean it up for me," added Penny. "Or take off twenty dollars."

"No problem," promised Zibby. "I'll get the maid doll on the job right away!"

Nonetheless, after hanging up the phone, she did not return to the dollhouse, but went downstairs to watch TV. After a half hour, a soft rain began to fall. By the time it grew dark outside, the rain was falling harder, pounding the roof of the Thornes' blue house. When Zibby's mom called to say that Charlotte was going to have to stay overnight at the hospital for observation, the rain was slashing through the darkness like a scythe.

"But will she be all right, Mom?" asked Zibby urgently.

"I'm sure she will," replied Nell. "But the gash was deeper than we thought at first, and she's lost a lot of blood. The doctors want to keep an eye on her until tomorrow."

"Oh, Mom, tell her I'm really, really sorry. I feel terrible."

"But it was no one's fault, honey. That's the nature of accidents." Nell's voice was reassuring. "But I'll be sure to tell her. Now, sweetheart, I'll be home in another hour or two. Are you all right alone? Shall I call Grammy and Gramps to come get you?"

Zibby looked out at the dark night and driving rain. She felt lonely and unsettled. But she wanted to clean up the dollhouse to give to Penny first thing in the morning. "I'll be okay here," she told her mom. "I'll wait till you get home."

As soon as she hung up the phone there was a crash of thunder that shook the house, and then the lights went out. The lightning that split the night outside illuminated the kitchen where Zibby sat at the table.

A power failure. From time to time the power would go out during a storm, but, always before, her mom had been home, and her dad, too, and it was fun, an adventure. Her dad would light candles and Nell and Zibby would make popcorn the old-fashioned way, in a pot held over the flame of the gas stove. The three of them would sit together and eat popcorn and Nell would tell stories about when she was a girl. Somehow her mom's childhood, right here in Carroway in this very same house, and not especially different from her own, seemed magical to Zibby. She knew the names of Nell's old friends who had once lived on this same street. She loved the story of how Nell had schemed to make the boy she liked ask her to the homecoming dance. She was sad when Nell's schnauzer puppy was hit by a car. She was indignant when Nell got in trouble with a teacher. "I wish I'd lived back then," Zibby had told Nell once. "I'd have been your friend."

Nell laughed. "Way back then, huh? You make me feel ancient. But I'd have loved to know you."

Her dad was great at devising quizzes for Zibby and Nell. The names of all the presidents. The state capitals. The rivers of South America. Five things you could eat that grew in the desert.

It had been cozy and companionable when her parents were with her when the lights went out. But now Zibby was alone. She wasn't even sure where the candles were. Her dad had been in charge of the candles.

Zibby got up and wandered around the kitchen and tiny pantry in the dark, waiting for bolts of lightning to light her way. She found a flashlight in one cupboard, but no batteries. She found a box of skinny little birthday cake candles in rainbow colors and a box of matches. She didn't have a cake to stick the candles in. What could she use instead?

Her eye fell on the little jade plant on the windowsill above the kitchen sink. She lifted it down and stuck candles into the dirt. Then she struck a match and lit one. She used the lit candle to light the others, just as she'd seen her mom do on birthday cakes. The candles flickered in a circle around the jade plant. Zibby carried her makeshift lantern to the table and sat down. She felt an unaccountable urge to go upstairs to the dollhouse, but ignored it. She couldn't watch TV without electricity, or listen to music, but she could read. So she pulled her mom's morning newspaper over and read the comics and advice columns. Then, resolutely, she waded through national news. She kept checking the clock and thinking she heard her mom's car in the driveway. But Nell didn't return and the skinny little candles eventually burned down to nubs of wax.

What could she do now? She wasn't about to sit here in the dark. Zibby looked at the phone and decided to call Grammy and Gramps after all. Thank goodness telephones didn't operate on electricity.

She dialed, listened to the ringing, waited — but

no one answered. Slowly she hung up. Now what? She looked around the dark room. Then she remembered the big, red, heart-shaped candle that Amy had given her as a going-away present, even though Amy herself was the one who was going away. Zibby had given Amy a photo album.

Zibby groped for the handrail and started up the stairs. Again she felt the urge to go to the dollhouse, and this time a whisper in her head, almost a thought — but louder. *Come and play.*

Zibby pushed the thought away and hurried down the hall. The house felt different in the dark. Bigger. Possibly threatening. *But that's just silly,* she told herself. It was just the darkness making her nervous.

Without trouble, she found the heart candle on her bookcase. It sat on a thick round holder of glass. She hadn't intended to burn it at all, because that would ruin its shape. But this was an emergency.

The first match she struck flickered out before it caught the wick, but the second match burned brightly. Zibby lit the candle and set it on the glass holder atop her desk.

Light!

And in the light, something awful.

The doll in the iron-gray dress sat now on the roof of the dollhouse, leaning back against the tiny brick chimney. Zibby's breath caught in her throat. She *knew* the doll had been right on the floor where Penny had tossed it. She knew it. And no one but Zibby herself had been in her bedroom since then.

Zibby's hand trembled as she lifted the heart candle in its thick glass holder and walked slowly over to the dollhouse. She wasn't sure whether it was more frightening to think that someone unknown — someone perhaps still hiding in the dark house — had entered her room and moved the doll, or that the doll herself had somehow climbed up onto the dollhouse roof.

*It couldn't be either,* she told herself desperately. It had to be something else. Maybe Charlotte had managed to run into her room, somehow, and move the doll before she'd fallen in the bathroom. And then Zibby just hadn't noticed the doll earlier. Or some other, perfectly innocent, explanation that hadn't occurred to her yet. She took a deep breath and plucked the grim-faced doll off the roof — and felt a stinging across her palm as if her hand had been struck. She dropped the doll and at the same time her hand gripping the glass candleholder dipped, toppling the red wax heart onto the pile of dolls.

The candle's flame caught the dry, old fabric of one of the dresses and a little flame grew while Zibby rubbed her aching hand and stared at it. In a panic, she grabbed the empty doll sack and pressed it hard down onto the flame, extinguishing it. Then she edged over to the desk for the box of matches. She lit the red candle again and assessed the damage.

The frown-faced doll lay on the floor, the skirt of her long, gray dress askew. Zibby lifted the sack off the pile of dolls to inspect the damage. Thank goodness, she noted, the flame had not damaged the rug. It had only singed the mother doll's green sleeve.

Then she froze. Was that a noise she heard downstairs? Was there a prowler in the house with her, after all?

She gulped in a great big breath, listening. Then with a quick puff she blew out the candle. She mustn't let him see the light.

Then the noise from downstairs came again — and with it her mom's welcome voice. "Zibby? I'm home!"

Abandoning the dolls, the dollhouse, the candle, the bedroom, the fear of prowlers, Zibby tore downstairs and into Nell's embrace. "Oh, Mom! I'm so glad you're home."

"And I'm glad to be home." Nell tiredly shook back her wet ponytail. "Have you been sitting in the dark, honey? Let's get some candles lit!"

"I looked, but all I could find were birthday candles."

"Oh, poor Zibby. You should have called Grammy and Gramps."

"I did, but no one answered."

"Hmm, I wonder if the phone lines are down? There's an incredible wind out there."

Nell opened the cupboard next to the refrigerator and reached up high. "Here we are!" She brought down two white tapers in brass holders. The rain beat down outside, drumming on the roof. The wind roared. Zibby was so glad to have her mom home, the weirdness with the doll upstairs receded and seemed almost something she'd only imagined.

Nell crossed the room to the stove, turned on the gas, and held the candle to the flame. Then, without warning, the back door blew open in a gust of wet wind and the gas flame flared, burning Nell's hand and wrist as she held the candles. She dropped them with a yell of pain. Zibby flew to slam and lock the door, and then just as suddenly as the lights had gone off when the power failed, they came back on. The kitchen light blazed overhead like a sunburst.

"Oh, Mom, are you okay?" cried Zibby.

Nell had rushed to the sink and was running cold water over the burn. She grimaced. "I'll live." She examined her reddened wrist. "This is certainly our night for accidents, isn't it?"

With a flash of foreboding, Zibby remembered the mother doll's singed sleeve, and the baby doll in the bathtub.

Accidents? Or something worse?

# Chapter 10

## *Primrose (1919)*

Up in the nursery there had been lots of toys for Primrose to play with. She had a rocking horse with a mane of real horsehair. She had shelves full of puzzles, spinning tops, wooden animals, and fairy-tale books. She had building bricks and roller skates, and games of checkers, jackstraw, and old maid. Best of all, she had a wooden bed for her dolls, and then there were the dolls themselves — baby dolls in bibs, fine lady dolls in lacy dresses, and even a tiny doll from Japan, wearing a silk kimono. Her father and mother had brought that doll back from their last long trip.

But in Miss Honeywell's schoolroom, Primrose was permitted very few toys. Most of her things had been left behind in the nursery for the baby twins to grow into. Primrose had brought her Japanese doll along, and her favorite baby doll with the wooden doll bed.

And she'd brought her games — though Miss Honeywell never wanted to play, and so the games gathered dust on the bottom shelf. Primrose had also brought her skates along, hoping that Miss Honeywell would take her out to the park, where she would be able to soar along the paths as she had on outings with Nanny Shanks — but Miss Honeywell said that skating wasn't ladylike. The only time they went to the park together was when Miss Honeywell wanted Primrose to gather plant samplings for her botany scrapbook. Little girls and boys on skates whizzed past her, shouting and laughing while Primrose knelt resentfully by the bushes, collecting leaves.

On the day of the first snow of the year, Primrose was sitting at the table in the schoolroom trying to memorize the major rivers of the world. She had a globe in front of her, and was writing down the names of the rivers on her blank map. Miss Honeywell sat across the table, writing a letter to her invalid sister in Philadelphia. Miss Honeywell's handwriting was sharp and clear, unlike Primrose's round, uneven script. Whenever Primrose's handwriting grew too uneven, Miss Honeywell smacked her palms with a ruler and made her write the whole page over again.

Primrose was trying hard to write the names of the rivers clearly. If only they weren't such long, hard names! She heard the clock on the landing chime ten o'clock, and remembered wistfully how Nanny Shanks would always bring her some milk and cinnamon toast — or hot chocolate when the day was cold — at this time of morning. Probably right now the little twins were sitting in the sunny nursery at their little table, sipping hot chocolate and eating toast. While here she was, working hard, and no chance of a break until lunchtime. Two more hours of geography — it was too much to bear.

Primrose's eyes filled with tears, but she dashed them away. Miss Honeywell hated tears. "If you want to cry, I'll give you something to cry about," she would say coolly, and out would come her ever-present ruler, ready to smack. "Young ladies must exhibit self-control."

She sighed and glanced over at the window yearningly — then drew in her breath. "Oh, look!" she cried before she could stop herself. "It's snowing!"

She pushed back her chair in excitement, but before she could leap up to run to the window to watch the soft, fluffy flakes falling past, Miss Honeywell's cold voice — colder than snow — stopped her.

"Sit down, young lady. When you have finished memorizing the names and locations of the rivers, you may get up from the table."

"Oh, but Miss Honeywell — it's the first snow of the year . . ."

"The snow will wait." Miss Honeywell frowned, then looked back down at the letter she was writing.

*Maybe it won't wait! Maybe it will melt before I ever learn all these stupid rivers!* thought Primrose furiously. But she forced herself to stay in her seat. From time to time she glanced over at the governess, and imagined the bookcase behind her tipping forward, tipping . . . tipping . . . until — CRASH — it fell straight over onto Miss Honeywell, flattening her like a pancake.

How could something like that be rigged up? Primrose stared at the bookcase, thinking, but couldn't figure it out. *We'd need a little earthquake or something,* she thought. *That would do it.* Then she imagined the snow falling and falling, until a huge snowbank surrounded the house. Then, somehow, she would get Miss Honeywell to come to the window — how? Because an interesting specimen of bird had just perched on the tree outside? — and then, WHAM!, a giant push, and down would go Miss Honeywell into the snow. Deep, over her head, knocked out cold. No one would find her body till spring. *Oh, my goodness,* Primrose imagined herself saying. *So that's where she went off to? I'm afraid I never noticed a thing. I was too busy memorizing all those rivers.*

Fantasies like these often helped to pass the long mornings of lessons, but certainly didn't help her learn geography. Primrose sighed again and looked back down at her map. After a few more minutes, Miss Honeywell left the table and went into her bedroom for another sheet of writing paper. Primrose saw her chance.

She dashed over to the window and stood, transfixed. The snow was beautiful. It drifted silently, thickly, the flakes looking heavy and soft. Already the ground was covered. She heard a shout, and there, around the side of the house, came Nanny Shanks, pulling the twins on their little sled. Poppy was clutching the sides of the wooden sled, her little face tipped up to the sky, grinning. Basil roared with laughter, patting his little mittened hands together. Nanny Shanks stopped and bent down to show the babies how to make a snowball. Primrose longed to grab her red wool coat and mittens and run outside to join them.

"I assume you have finished your work or you would not have left the table, am I correct, young miss?" Miss Honeywell had returned.

Primrose started back to her seat. "Oh, let's go outside, please," she begged.

"Not finished yet, I see." Miss Honeywell stood over Primrose and inspected her map. "Hold out your hands, then. You leave me no choice." She withdrew her ruler from her long skirt pocket.

Rebelliously Primrose put her hands behind her back.

"Hold out your hands, or it's into the closet with you!" Miss Honeywell never raised her voice, but it had the power of a shout.

The closet. Primrose hated the closet. That was where Miss Honeywell locked her from time to time for bad behavior. The last time Primrose had been in the closet was last week after she had poured cold water into the center of Miss Honeywell's bed, soaking her mattress. She had been in the closet for two hours that time, huddled in the dark among the coats.

She held out her hands, wincing as Miss Honeywell struck the ruler across her palms six times.

"I hate you, old Honeywell!" muttered Primrose, blinking back tears of pain and rage.

"That's Sweet Miss Honeywell, to you," snapped the governess. "Now it's back to work with you. And this time I don't want anymore — "

A clamor from the courtyard below stopped her, and this time Miss Honeywell was the one who peered out the window. Primrose edged over to look as well.

A long, black, shiny automobile had driven in, with the Parsons' chauffeur at the wheel. A dark-haired woman in an elegant red cape was helped out by the driver. A fair-haired man in a black coat emerged next.

"It's Mama and Papa!" squealed Primrose. "I didn't know they were coming home today!" She glared at Miss Honeywell. "You might have told me, you know."

The governess pressed her lips together, frowning out the window. "I expected them later tonight. You would have been in bed," she finally said. "All right, young miss. Don't just stand there. Go at once to your room and put on a nice dress. Your green and blue gingham will be just the thing."

For once Primrose and Miss Honeywell were in agreement. Primrose skipped off to her room in delight, almost forgetting her still stinging palms. The green and blue dress was one her father had bought on his last trip. She had not had any chance to wear it till now. But Miss Honeywell believed that children should see their parents only when properly attired and on best behavior, so the dress was brought out of the wardrobe at last. Primrose changed swiftly from her brown woolen school dress, hoping her parents would call her to come down even before they visited the babies in the nursery. Perhaps Nanny Shanks had not returned from their outing yet, in which case she *would* get to see her parents first. She jumped on one foot and then the other while Miss Honeywell buttoned the green and blue dress up the back.

"Stand still, Primrose," snapped the governess.

"Hurry, hurry. I can't wait any longer!"

"You'll have to." And it seemed to Primrose that the governess's fingers moved more slowly than ever along the row of buttons.

Primrose bit her lip. She resolved to tell her parents everything — about the closet, the ruler, the clothespin — about her unhappy daily life with this horrid woman. They would send Miss Honeywell away on the spot and let Primrose go back to Nanny Shanks.

There was a tap on the door and Miss Honeywell opened it to the uniformed maid, who dropped a brief curtsy and said, "Captain and Mrs. Parson would like to see Miss Primrose in the front parlor at once."

"Hooray!" yelled Primrose and darted past Miss Honeywell and the maid. She pelted down the stairs, ignoring Miss Honeywell's hissed rebuke. She flew across the grand entrance hall, her feet slipping on the marble floor, to the parlor. The door was closed. She tapped twice, then flung the door wide. "Papa! Mama! Oh, I've missed you so much! You've been gone for such a long time!"

Primrose's parents smiled and held out their arms for a hug. She rubbed her cheek against the rough wool of her papa's jacket, inhaled the wonderful, flowery perfume her mama wore. She wished she could stay with them, be here like this forever, and have nasty Miss Honeywell just disappear in a flash of smoke. But after a moment, Papa set her away from him and patted her shoulder. He looked over her head at Miss Honeywell.

"Come in, Miss Honeywell. Come in and join us. We'll want you to tell us about Primrose's progress."

"She's doing well enough, sir," said Miss Honeywell. "We're studying geography, literature, mathematics, and French every day."

Mama stroked Primrose's hair. "What a big girl you're becoming," she murmured. *This is when I should tell them,* thought Primrose. *Tell them about horrible Miss Honeywell.* But she just stood still under her mama's stroking hand and remained silent. She could feel the governess's eyes on her. *You want me to keep quiet, don't you, old witch?* she thought. *So no one will know how mean you are. Well, I'm going to tell!* Then she wondered whether Miss Honeywell would tell her parents about the practical jokes Primrose had played on the governess. She knew her mama, especially, would not like to hear that Primrose had done such things.

"Getting big, that's good, but not *too* big, I hope," said Papa with a smile. "Not too big for the presents we've brought you!"

"Oh, no, Papa. I'm never going to be too big for presents." The moment was gone. She would have to wait till later to tell them about Miss Honeywell. Sometime when they were alone.

"Come upstairs with us, then. Up to your schoolroom. I've asked John and Charles to carry up the surprises we have for you. They should be ready by now."

John was the butler and Charles was the chauffeur. Whatever Mama and Papa had brought her must be pretty large and pretty heavy! Primrose, excited by her parents' return and by the thought of the gifts waiting upstairs, hurried ahead of the adults. Normally Miss Honeywell would have admonished her to slow down and walk like a lady. But with Primrose's parents there, the governess held her tongue.

Primrose peeked around the door of the schoolroom, and caught her breath. There by the windows stood a dollhouse, the most beautiful dollhouse she had ever seen.

"Oh, Papa! Mama! It's exactly what I hoped for! It's even more beautiful than I ever imagined!"

The dollhouse was half as tall as she was herself, and had a brown-shingled roof and two brick chimneys. It had a front porch with little steps leading up to it and a front door with a panel of brilliant-hued stained glass. It had three stories and a tower room. Papa walked over to it proudly and showed Primrose how the front of the house opened out in two sections to reveal eight main rooms — four upstairs and four downstairs, with one large attic and two smaller rooms in the tower. The walls were all papered with tiny prints, and the little floorboards were polished. Miniature chandeliers hung from the ceilings.

"Oh, Papa, Mama," whispered Primrose. "How perfectly perfect!"

"That's not all," laughed Papa. He reached for a large box Primrose had not noticed on the schoolroom table. "There's still this to open." And he pulled his silver penknife out of his pocket to help her with the cord.

She opened the box as fast as she could, and gasped at the wrapped bundles of dollhouse furniture inside.

"Papa picked out the house for you, Primrose," said Mama. "But I had all the fun of shopping for it! We went all over London and Paris, and I searched all the shops for the best home furnishings. Little tables and chairs and couches and carpets — even a gramophone, Primrose. It's darling! And wait till you see the dolls."

Mama dug through the big box until she found a smaller box tied with a ribbon.

"Look," she said, opening the ribbon, "here's the family that lives in the house!"

Primrose gazed in wonder at the dolls. They were small — of course they would have to be to live in the dollhouse. The father doll was no more than six inches tall, and the mother was slightly shorter. There were four children — two boys and two girls. One of the girls had brown braids like Primrose's. There were three servants, one man and two women. There were also two tiny baby dolls wrapped in green blankets.

"Oh, Mama! They're twins just like Basil and Poppy."

"And there is one more doll I bought separately," said Mama, peering into the big box. "She must be here somewhere —"

"Oh, Mama, this is all so wonderful. Will you stay here and help me set everything up?" asked Primrose, delight making her voice squeak. This was better than Christmas. Better than her birthday.

Mama abandoned her search for the other doll. "Well, dear, I'm afraid Papa and I don't really have much time to stay at home. We're here really just on a stopover to see you and the babies — but we're leaving again . . ."

"Oh, Mama, no!"

"Now, dear, be reasonable. Your papa's work takes

him all around the world. And as his wife it is my duty to go with him."

Primrose turned back to the beautiful dollhouse, but already some of the joy had gone out of the gift. She glanced up at Miss Honeywell. The governess's face wore a smile, and she was nodding as if agreeing with everything Mama said.

"Well, Mama and Papa, thank you for this lovely gift," Primrose said suddenly. "But I doubt I shall *ever* be able to play with it. Miss Honeywell, you see, doesn't believe in playing."

Papa turned his piercing gaze on the governess. "Really, Miss Honeywell? Well, that is nonsense. Of course Primrose must have playtime." He held up his hand when the governess began to speak. "Now, I want you to be sure to schedule in playtime every day after her lessons are done. Is that clear?"

"Yes, sir, of course," said Miss Honeywell sweetly. "I have no problem with play at all, as long as her lessons are finished first."

Papa turned away satisfied, but Mama gave Miss Honeywell a sharp look. "Be sure that her lessons do not overtire her, Miss Honeywell," Mama said. "She must be finished by three o'clock every day and have weekends free."

Miss Honeywell frowned, but her voice was pleasant. "Yes, ma'am. Of course."

Primrose smiled. She would wait till she was alone with her mama to tell her everything else about Miss Honeywell.

But there was no time alone at all. Primrose went with her parents to the nursery to see the babies, but Nanny Shanks was bubbling over with news of how Basil could crawl and Poppy was pulling herself up already, and there was no chance to talk in private. Then Primrose ate dinner downstairs with her parents that night, sitting around the elegant dining room table and being waited upon by the servants. But Miss Honeywell joined them as well. And after dinner her mama came along to her bedroom to kiss her good night, but had to hurry away because she and Papa were going out to the theater.

And in the morning they were gone.

For a while Primrose was so sad she couldn't concentrate on her lessons, and she had her hands smacked so many times, her palms seemed to be permanently stinging. She was so sad, she couldn't even play with the dollhouse, though Miss Honeywell was careful to stop lessons punctually at three o'clock, ringing her little bell to indicate when Primrose might close her books and leave the table. She was so sad that her steps felt weighted down and she dragged herself through the long winter days with nothing to cheer her up. She wanted her mama and papa to stay home. It wasn't enough that they should bring her fine gifts. She needed them to be home.

She sat slumped over the schoolbooks, not even bothering to try to add the numbers Miss Honeywell had set in columns on the page. And when the governess appeared at her side, hands on hips, Primrose didn't even look up.

"Primrose Parson!" snapped Miss Honeywell. "You have been sitting here for an hour already and have not done a single sum. Now you stand up, young miss. Girls of good breeding must learn to be obedient. I don't know why you won't make an effort. You're practically begging me to correct you. Now hold out your hands." The governess reached for the ruler she never let far out of her grasp.

But suddenly Primrose rebelled. She clenched her hands — palms still stinging from the last assault from Miss Honeywell's ruler — into fists. "No!" she yelled at the top of her voice. "I won't! You can't make me! You're horrid and ugly and mean, mean, mean — and I hate you! I hope you die!"

In an instant Miss Honeywell had grabbed Primrose and pulled her right out of her chair. She took Primrose by the shoulders and shook her so hard, Primrose thought she heard her brains rattling. Then she dragged her across the schoolroom to the closet — the dreaded dark closet.

"Oh, please, Miss Honeywell, don't lock me in," cried Primrose helplessly as the governess opened the door and shoved her inside. Primrose crumpled onto the floor and lay there sobbing. She heard the key turn in the lock, and Miss Honeywell's voice outside.

"You will stay in there until you can behave yourself."

Primrose pressed her lips together and made herself stop crying. It did no good to cry.

Promptly at three o'clock the key turned in the lock and Miss Honeywell opened the door. Primrose had been napping on the hard floor of the closet. She awoke groggily.

"Out you come, you naughty girl. Time to come out and play," said the governess.

"Play?" Primrose struggled to her feet. She wanted to run to Nanny Shanks for comfort, that's what she wanted. She didn't feel in the least like playing at anything.

"It's three o'clock. Time your mama said was playtime. So start playing."

"I'd rather go up to the nursery and see the twins," Primrose began in a soft voice, but Miss Honeywell cut her off.

"It's time to play, so play you shall. You haven't even touched the nice dollhouse your mama and papa brought all the way from Europe. You should be ashamed of yourself."

*Miss Honeywell is so mean, she can even make playtime feel like a punishment,* thought Primrose morosely as she walked over to the dollhouse. Her legs felt shaky from being cramped on the closet floor for so long. She knelt by the house and, feeling Miss Honeywell's angry eyes on her back, opened the latch and swung open the front.

She began unwrapping the furnishings her mama had packed into the box, and setting them in the various rooms. Soon she became absorbed, and forgot about Miss Honeywell. After a while she remembered, and glanced over her shoulder to see what the governess was doing. She was on the other side of the big room, settled into the armchair with a heavy, dull-looking book open on her knees.

Perking up, Primrose turned back to the dollhouse. She finished arranging the furniture, then untied the red ribbon around the box of dolls. One by one she lifted them out and settled them into their new house. "Let's see," she said to herself. "You'll be the mama and you'll be the papa, and you're away on a long, long trip — as always." She set the two parent dolls behind her on the floor. Then she picked out one of the servant dolls. "You'll be the nanny, and you'll live up in the nursery with the two little babies." She arranged the doll with the two babies up in the big bedroom. Then she set that room up as a nursery, with cribs and high chairs, and a tiny rocking horse by the window. She put three of the four children dolls into the nursery, but set one of the girl dolls up in the attic. "That's the schoolroom," she murmured to herself. "The nanny and the children are so happy in the nursery. While their big sister is studying in the schoolroom, they get to go on outings and eat snacks and play with all their lovely toys. Sometimes the nanny even takes them to the circus!"

Primrose had the idea that she could draw circus animals on her art paper and cut them out with scissors and make a circus for the dolls to go to. She crossed the room to her shelf of supplies and brought the scissors and paper to the floor by the dollhouse. She spent the next hour drawing elephants and horses and acrobats and coloring them with her bright colored pencils. This was much more fun than coloring in rivers on a geography map! For the first time since her parents' visit, Primrose felt her heart lifting with the joy of play. She glanced from time to time over at Miss Honeywell, but the governess was absorbed in her book and was, for once, leaving Primrose in peace.

"Now the nanny is taking the children to the circus," she murmured to herself, "but the little ones say, 'wait, wait, we want our big sister to come along.'" Primrose reached for the girl doll with the brown braids like her own.

"The poor big sister lives up in the attic with a horrible mean governess," she whispered, and looked at the remaining dolls to select one to be governess. But none looked nasty enough. Then she remembered that her mother had said there was another doll, and she started rooting through the remaining furnishings until she found it. The box was small, and tied simply with string.

Inside lay a grown-up doll wearing a gray dress. She was a little bit larger than all the other dolls, even larger than the six-inch father doll. She almost seemed too big to live in the dollhouse, but it was the expression on her face that made Primrose lift her out and place her in the attic. Her little painted face wore a frown just like Miss Honeywell's.

"The big sister lived in the schoolroom with the nasty governess," whispered Primrose. "The girl was practically a prisoner. The governess locked her in the closet and beat her with a ruler all the time. When the nanny and children came to ask the girl along to the circus, the governess said no, she had to stay and do lessons." Primrose acted this out with the dolls, kneeling so she could reach the dollhouse attic.

"So the girl decided to get rid of the governess once and for all. The nanny and the little twins helped. They wrestled the nasty governess to the floor and dragged her over to the window."

Primrose arranged the little dolls around the larger doll and scooted them across the dollhouse attic to the windows. She found that by pressing her fingernail into the groove at the base of the window she was able to lift the sash. "They opened the window," she murmured. "The governess cried out, 'oh, help, help,' but they didn't listen to her. They pushed her out with a mighty shove — WHAM!"

Primrose pushed the governess doll through the window and let her drop onto the floor below. "And that was the end of her," she said with satisfaction.

"Primrose Parson!" snapped her real governess's voice just behind her. "What in the world are you doing? If you break those dolls, your papa will be very angry. If you can't play with them carefully, you won't be able to play with them at all."

Primrose obediently picked up the fallen doll and placed her carefully back into the dollhouse. But her cheeks were flushed and her eyes twinkled for the first time in ages. Getting rid of Miss Honeywell was a game she knew she would play again.

# Chapter 11

Penny and Jude knocked on the kitchen door of Zibby's house the next morning after breakfast. Nell, her burned wrist wrapped lightly in a gauze dressing, had already left to meet Aunt Linnea and Uncle David at the hospital. They were bringing Charlotte home. Zibby got up slowly from the table where she was poking at a fried egg and went to the door.

"Oh, Zibby," said Penny excitedly through the screen door. "Wasn't that storm last night totally cool? You should see our backyard! An elm tree crashed down and just missed the garage by inches! Come on over, okay? Like right now? We'll build a clubhouse in the branches and —"

Zibby unlatched the screen door and opened it. "Come on in," she murmured, interrupting Penny's chatter.

"Is this a bad time or something?" asked Jude. "You don't look very happy to see us."

"No, it's okay." Zibby hesitated, then told them what had happened to Charlotte the night before. She did not mention her uneasiness about the dollhouse.

"Was there a lot of blood?" asked Penny, horrified.

"Penny, you are so gross," hissed Jude. Then she looked hard at Zibby. "You look kind of sick. Are you all right?"

"I just feel weird. And tired. I didn't sleep very well."

Jude nodded. "When will your cousin come home from the hospital?"

"Soon. My mom went over to my aunt's house, and then they're going to go get Charlotte. They'll all be coming here for lunch."

"Well, how about if Penny and I go back home now," said Jude, "and you just come over later when you feel like it."

"Yeah, and I'll bring my tools," Zibby said, smiling at Jude. It was nice that she seemed to understand Zibby's mood. Amy had been like that, too. "Amy and I were going to build a clubhouse, even though we didn't exactly have a club," Zibby added. "Do you two have one?"

"Not yet. But we can start one," Penny spoke up. "That's what I was trying to tell you, Zibby. The tree that fell in our yard will be just perfect. It's like a tree house already."

"Yeah, it'll be great — until Noddy gets out his chain saw," said Jude. "I bet you your dad will have that tree reduced to lumber before we get home."

"Jude!" squealed Penny. "He will not! I told him we wanted to play there."

"Oh. Well, in that case, no problem." Jude rolled her eyes for Zibby's benefit. "I'm telling you, Penny is queen over at our house. She gets what she wants, make no mistake."

Penny tossed her braids. "Well, I just know how to ask for things, that's all. In fact," she said, grinning at Zibby, "my mom wants to come over and see your dollhouse. To see if we should buy it, she said. I told her it's totally perfect, but she still wants to check it out. Is it okay if she comes after lunch?"

"Yeah, I guess so," said Zibby slowly. "I'll call you when Charlotte and her family go home." She wondered whether she should tell Penny about the weird things going on with the dollhouse and with the doll in the gray dress. But if she did, then Penny might not want to buy it. And selling the house to Penny was one sure way of getting rid of it — and getting her eighty-five bucks back, too.

She frowned, remembering the old woman at the miniature show who had sold her the dollhouse. She remembered the look on the old woman's face as Zibby had handed over her money. The old woman had look pleased — and relieved.

No refunds, no returns.

What had the old woman known about the old dollhouse that she hadn't told Zibby?

"Zibby?!" Penny sounded impatient.

Zibby pushed thoughts of the woman out of her head and looked at Penny. "Sorry. What did you say?"

"I *said,* when you come over, do you want to see my trolls? They're the ones who will live in the dollhouse once it's mine."

"Oh, yeah." She sighed. "Later. I'll see them when I come over. Right now I'm going to go up and start cleaning the dollhouse."

Jude looked at her closely and opened the screen door. "We won't start the club without you," she promised. She started down the path with Penny following.

"'Bye," said Zibby, and closed the door. She was glad they were gone. She needed to think. All night after the storm she'd tossed and turned in bed, too aware of the dollhouse looming in the corner to rest peacefully. She walked upstairs now, and stood in front of it.

It looked so innocent, sitting there. It had been beautiful once, she supposed, and could probably be made beautiful again with a little time and carpentry skill. Penny wanted it cleaned up, and Zibby had decided to get busy scrubbing and polishing. But one look at the grim-faced doll in the gray dress made her think again. It was sitting on her windowsill now, facing the room. This time Zibby wasn't even surprised, though she knew very well she had left the doll on the floor with the others. She felt as if it were watching her with its little painted eyes.

Her mom had not come in and moved the doll. Charlotte certainly hadn't.

Zibby reached for the doll, holding her breath. Gingerly, she carried it downstairs, upside down, hanging by the skirt of its long, gray dress. She wrapped it up in the sports pages of yesterday's newspaper and took it outside to the brown plastic trash bins behind the house. This doll was bad news. She wouldn't sell it to Penny with the other dolls in the dollhouse. And she sure didn't want it around *her* house anymore.

"Rest in peace," she said, and tossed the newspaper-wrapped bundle into the bin. She slammed the brown plastic lid on hard, pressing down until she heard it latch.

*There.* Zibby turned away from the bins and walked back to the house. She sat on the front porch and tried to get into one of the mystery books Charlotte's brother, Owen, had given her for her birthday. But the mystery of the dollhouse clouded her mind and made concentration difficult. Finally Nell's car drove into the driveway. Aunt Linnea's van turned in right behind her. Zibby ran to greet them.

Charlotte had a bandage on her head and looked pale. "I had to have sixteen stitches," she announced. "That's more than you had when you cut your foot at the beach."

Zibby had had eleven stitches three years ago after gashing her foot on a piece of glass buried in the sand. They'd been vacationing at the beach by Lake Pymatuning. It had been a happy time, though the rush to the emergency room hadn't made anyone happy. Zibby's dad had held her on his lap the whole time the doctor was stitching the gash.

Zibby pushed away the memory. "Okay," she conceded brightly. "The one who has the most stitches is the gold medal winner."

"The one who has the most stitches gets the biggest ice-cream sundae after lunch," added Owen, carrying in a bag from the grocery store. He flung his arm over his younger sister's shoulders.

"Yum," said Zibby. "That's the kind of pain relief I like."

"You'll get fat," Charlotte said, predictably. "And you'll get zits."

"I'll eat your share if you can't manage it," Zibby retorted. She knew Charlotte adored every flavor of ice cream ever invented. Before she had become so ladylike, she could dig into a gallon as well as anybody.

"Then let's go eat," said Nell, and led the way into the house.

First they settled Charlotte on the couch. Zibby brought her cousin a glass of lemonade while Nell and Aunt Linnea made tuna sandwiches. Uncle David ate quickly, then rushed off to work. He had taken time off to see his daughter home from the hospital, but wasn't free to stay for lunch. "Don't feel bad, Uncle David," Zibby teased. "I'll eat an extra sundae for you."

Charlotte sighed. "Oh, Zibby. You've really got to start thinking about your figure."

"I just let you think about it for me," said Zibby. "Saves me the trouble." She turned away, determined to ignore Charlotte. Her cousin was already back to sounding like her usual self. *That was good,* Zibby told herself. *It meant she hadn't been hurt* too *badly.*

Owen threw himself into the big leather armchair where Zibby's dad had always sat. Owen's long legs stuck out almost as far as her dad's had, Zibby noticed. She'd always had to step over them to get by. She tried to step carefully over Owen's legs the same way, but he raised them and tried to trip her.

She gave him a kick and he grabbed her and tickled her. They both fell onto the floor, laughing. Charlotte watched from the couch with a frown. "Really, Zibby," she muttered. "You act like a child. Both of you do. It's really dumb."

Owen and Zibby nudged each other in silent commentary. Aunt Linnea came in and fluttered around, worrying that they were being too loud, afraid they were disturbing Charlotte, wondering whether it was too warm, and should they turn on the fan or open all the windows . . .

"Sit down, Mom," Owen begged. "Char's okay."

Nell served the sandwiches in the living room so they could all sit near Charlotte, and Charlotte regaled them with stories about her overnight stay in the hospital. She'd missed the blackout, she said, looking disappointed, because the hospital had emergency generators that kicked in immediately.

"Good thing, though," said Nell. "Think of the people hooked up to respirators, or the little babies in incubators. The hospital depends on steady electric power."

"It wasn't so great," Zibby said. "I was here all alone, looking for candles. It was creepy." Then she remembered why it was creepy, and remembered that Penny would be bringing her mother soon to check out the dollhouse. She finished her ice cream in a hurry and left her mom and aunt chatting with Charlotte and Owen while she went up to her room to clean up the dollhouse.

In the upstairs hallway, she heard a soft ringing. She stopped. Was it a real bell, or the one in her head? It rang again.

And when her palms started stinging, Zibby knew. The bell was in her head. And it was something to do with the dollhouse. Slowly, afraid, and yet needing to know, she walked into her room. The dollhouse looked to be just as she had left it — open, with the pile of dolls still lying on the rug. The sting in her palms intensified as she looked around the room. And then she saw it.

There on her desk was the doll in the gray dress.

Zibby froze. *Don't think you can get rid of me so easily, young miss,* it seemed to gloat.

After a minute, Zibby backed out of her room. This was impossible. The doll couldn't be there. *Couldn't* be. She had wrapped it securely in newspaper. She had carried it to the trash bins. She had heard the lid click into place. No one else had been home. No one had left the house to dig through the trash bin. No one could have found the doll and brought her back.

She stared at the doll on her desk. Then she turned and ran down the stairs as fast as she could, out the kitchen door and around to the trash bins. She jerked the lid off the one she had latched, and there was the wad of newspaper still rolled up as she'd left it. She held her breath and unwrapped it.

Nothing. The newspaper was empty.

Terror welled in Zibby. Something was wrong, terribly wrong, about the doll. She had to get rid of it, and get rid of the house, too. She couldn't let Penny buy it. Not even to get her eighty-five dollars back. She felt a surge of anger at the old woman who had sold her the dollhouse. Had she known about the grim-faced doll? She must have known. *Thanks a lot, lady!*

She couldn't let her mom or Aunt Linnea or Charlotte see what she was going to do next. They would stop her. They wouldn't believe her about the dollhouse, how it had returned to her room from Nell's. How the nasty doll returned from the trash.

But first she had to call Penny and tell her the sale was off.

"I can't believe you would be so mean," cried Penny over the phone. Zibby gripped the receiver more tightly and tried to think of a good explanation.

"You said I could buy it!"

"It's — um — not that I don't want you to have it," Zibby said quickly, wrapping the cord around her hand nervously. "It's that — umm — my mom won't let me sell it." That was it. That was the perfect excuse. And it probably would even be true. "Really, I *wish* you could buy the dollhouse. More than anything. But my mom says absolutely not. She wants to keep the house as a — as an heirloom or something." Zibby knew she sounded nervous. She wasn't used to lying. "So tell your mom not to come over to see it. I mean, she could come see it if she wanted, but it's not for sale anymore. I'm *really* sorry, Penny." *At least that part is the truth!*

Penny seemed mollified, more sad than angry, by the time the girls hung up. Zibby hoped she'd still let her help build the clubhouse. That project sounded like fun, and would take her mind off the dollhouse. And how she was going to get rid of it.

Zibby waited. After lunch, Charlotte, drowsy from

painkillers, started falling asleep on the couch. Aunt Linnea and Owen led her out to the van and drove home. And Nell left to cater an afternoon tea party. She promised to be home before dinner.

As soon as the house was quiet, Zibby ran upstairs to her room. She bundled the sack of dolls into the dollhouse. Then, gingerly, hating to touch it, she picked up the doll in the gray dress, who still sat on the desk, and shoved it into the house, too. She closed up the house and latched it securely. Then she got her quilt, wrapped it around and under the house, and dragged the whole thing out into the hallway. She bumped it down the stairs, the quilt muting most of the noise as the big dollhouse thudded along. She dragged the dollhouse through the dining room, through the kitchen, then out the back door.

She left the bundle on the grass while she searched in the garage for her old red wagon. There it was, back by the wall. Zibby hadn't used it for years, but her dad had used it to hold gardening supplies.

Zibby had another use for it now. She heaved the quilt-covered house into the wagon, grunting with exertion, and started off down the driveway, then along the sidewalk. The perfect place to ditch the dollhouse was a ten-minute walk from her house, down by the river. She hurried along, hoping no one would stop her to ask her about the large, awkward cargo in her wagon. The house was heavy, and she strained to pull it up and down the hilly streets.

Carroway was an old town, settled by pioneers way back in the early 1800s — when Abe Lincoln was a boy, Grammy had told her. Carroway's Main Street stretched the entire length of town, with branching streets leading off into the wooded countryside. The town center was a square of buildings around a grassy green. There were three old churches and a much newer synagogue, four banks, an antique store, and the old town hall. The old town hall had become the Carroway Little Theater, where Aunt Linnea and Uncle David often performed in community plays. Owen also acted in plays from time to time. Charlotte herself had played Wendy two years ago in *Peter Pan,* hoisted high on wires and made to fly. The new town hall was on a side street, an awkward modern building of steel and concrete that squatted amidst the older buildings of brick and wood.

Behind the new town hall was a narrow lane that led down to the Carroway River, and this was where Zibby headed with the wagon. River access was usually from the end of Main Street, where a nice little dock and park drew business men and women on their lunch hour, children with sailboats and Frisbees after school, and teenagers on balmy evenings after dark. The lane where Zibby trudged led down to an area hidden by a bend in the river and shunned by most of Carroway's citizens. It was the town dump, an eyesore only partially hidden behind a wooden fence. Hills of dirt and rubble, metal and plastic towered over the broken-down appliances and furniture that lay strewn in valleys of brown river water.

Zibby trundled the dollhouse over to a puddle of brown water and unwrapped the quilt. Then she shoved the house off the wagon. It tipped straight into the mud, on its side. Satisfied, Zibby folded her quilt and turned her back on the dump. She pulled the wagon all the way home, trying to think what she'd tell her mom about the dollhouse. She decided to say she'd given it to Penny, and just hoped that Penny never said anything to the contrary.

At last she was home again, and went up to cool off in her air-conditioned bedroom with her mystery book. She was lighter-hearted than before. Whatever the mystery of the nasty doll was about, it was no longer her concern.

Or so she thought — until she walked into her bedroom and saw the house, not muddy at all, standing neatly in the corner as if it had never been away.

Zibby screamed. Then she clapped her hand over her mouth in terror. She narrowed her eyes. Through her fear came anger. This was going too far. *There must be a way to get rid of the house and the doll. There must be!*

Staring at the house, Zibby thought of what that

way must be. A way that would destroy the house completely, a way that would reduce it to nothing. If only there were time enough before her mother came home.

She unfolded the quilt to start all over again. Wrapping the house, lugging it down the stairs.

Zibby hated to touch the house now. If felt alive and malevolent to her. But she dragged it downstairs and out the back door again. Then she stood in the backyard, looking around. *Where would be the best place? What about the old brick patio behind the house?* It was still choked with weeds. Gardening had been her dad's chore — a chore he'd enjoyed. With him gone, Zibby and Nell rarely remembered. Gramps kept promising to come over and whip the yard into shape, but so far he hadn't had time.

The brick of the patio would keep the fire from spreading. *At least I hope so,* thought Zibby as she unwrapped the house, and threw her quilt far away from it onto the grass. She went into the garage and returned with a can of lighter fluid her mom used when lighting charcoal on the barbecue. She opened the nozzle and sprayed the fluid all over the dollhouse, watched it sink into the old, dry, thirsty wood. She soaked it well, until the entire can was empty. Then she ran back to the kitchen for the matches.

She was working quickly, trying not to think about the trouble she'd be in when her mom found out what she had done, trying not to think of how she could possibly explain. It seemed important, now that she'd decided on this course of action, to get it over with fast. *Get rid of the house and the doll,* she told herself. *Then worry about what comes next.*

As she lit the match and held it toward the house, ready to leap back at the first flame, she could see the gray cloth of the nasty doll's dress through one of the little upstairs windows.

"That's the end of you," she said aloud, and threw the match.

As the house flared up in a column of flame, she heard the bell tolling. Then she heard a terrible scream.

# Chapter 12

"What in the world are you doing?" screamed the voice behind her, and Zibby whirled around to see Jude, hands on hips, in the driveway. "I saw you throw the match! Are you crazy?" She ran to the hose looped next to the back door and cranked on the water. "Quick, you pyromaniac. We might still be able to save it —"

"No!" Zibby grabbed the hose out of Jude's hands. "Let it burn. I don't want it."

"I can't believe you! You are the most totally selfish person I ever met in my life." Tears streamed from Jude's eyes both from the billowing smoke and from anger. Zibby could barely see the other girl now through the thick, smoky haze. "Do you burn up *all* your toys when you don't feel like playing with them anymore? Didn't you ever stop to think that maybe some other kid would want your things — like Penny, for instance? She's all broken-up because your mom said you couldn't sell your dollhouse, and here you are, burning it to ashes. It was a beautiful thing — a work of art. And you've ruined it, all for *nothing!*"

"It's *not* for nothing," Zibby retorted. She was staring, grim-faced, at the crackling flames shooting out of all the little windows. The fire popped as the miniature brick chimney exploded. Jude lunged again for the hose, but Zibby fended her off. "Just let it burn," Zibby shouted. "I don't want it, and I don't want Penny to have it because —"

"— you're selfish and mean!" cried Jude.

"— because something's wrong with it." Zibby watched with satisfaction as the dollhouse roof collapsed.

"You are completely crazy." Jude turned away. "I'm going to tell. Kids like you should be locked away from normal people where they can't do any more damage."

"Wait, Jude —" The exhilaration of watching the house and the nasty doll burn began to ebb as the flames consumed the last of the old wooden structure and the summer breeze blew the smoke away. Zibby felt the first shiver of apprehension as she looked at the charred wreckage. Her mom would go berserk when she saw it. Zibby would have to think fast to come up with an explanation.

Would the truth work?

She pressed her lips together tightly. Who was she

kidding? They'd lock her away in a psychiatric hospital before she even finished.

Her mom's car turned into the driveway. Nell parked the car, then walked to the front door. She didn't seem to notice the smoke pall over the house.

Without another word, Jude started toward her. Nell went inside, and Jude rushed after her, up the steps of the porch and right inside without even knocking. Panicked, Zibby tore after Jude. She flung open the door and ran inside. Nell had started up the stairs, stooping to pick up a pile of folded laundry from the bottom step. Jude, climbing, directly behind her, was gibbering something about fire and crazy girls. Zibby, panting, barreled in right behind Jude. "Don't listen to her, Mom! Everything she says is totally lies."

Nell turned at the top of the stairs and shook her head. "Whoa, you two," she said. "You sound like a herd of buffalo."

"But she burned down her —"

Zibby raised her voice to drown out Jude's. "Jude just barged in our house without knocking! Can you believe it, Mom? Isn't that rude?"

Nell held out the pile of laundry as if to fend the girls off. "Hold everything. First of all, Zibby, would you mind introducing your friend? It's not that I mind having people race after me on the stairs, but at least I should know who they are."

Jude blinked and ducked her head. Zibby could tell she was embarrassed. *Well, good. She should be.* "This is Jude Jefferson, Mom," Zibby said hastily. "Um, and Jude — this is my mom, Nell Thorne. She —"

"How nice to meet you, Jude," Nell said pleasantly. She turned and started down the hallway. "So tell me, where did your family move here from?"

Zibby could see that Jude was desperate to tell Nell about the dollhouse, but her good manners prevailed. "We lived in Pennsylvania," she said. "But Noddy — my grandfather, I mean — bought the lumberyard here in town, and so we moved."

Zibby spoke up quickly, hoping to keep the conversation going. "Jude lives with her grandparents because her parents are in Africa. They're both doctors, Mom, helping to start up a new hospital there, isn't that neat? So Jude is spending the year with —"

"About Zibby's dollhouse," Jude interrupted. "I hate to tell you, but she —"

"And Jude has an aunt — that's Penny, Mom — who's *younger* than she is, can you believe it?" Zibby interrupted. "Just think how funny it would be if Aunt Linnea were only ten years old!"

They had been progressing slowly down the hall toward Zibby's room. Nell walked in now with the folded laundry and laid it on the bed. "I want you to put everything away neatly," she said to Zibby. "In fact, your whole room could use a good cleaning." Then she glanced over at Jude. "Now what's this you're trying to tell me about the dollhouse?"

Zibby squeezed her eyes shut and waited for the explosion. But Jude was silent. Zibby opened her eyes and looked at her. Jude was standing rigid, staring at the corner by the bookcase. Zibby stared, too.

The dollhouse was back.

"No," whispered Jude. Zibby saw that she was trembling.

"It's nothing, Mom," said Zibby quickly. "Jude just wanted to say — well, that she really likes my dollhouse. It's a work of art, she told me." Her voice was firm, as if a reasonable tone of voice might change what stood before their eyes.

Nell looked at them curiously, then shrugged. "It is a lovely house. Or at least, it would be if you cleaned it up."

"We will," said Zibby brightly. "We'll start right now. Right, Jude?"

Jude didn't answer. Nell left the room carrying the rest of the folded laundry.

Zibby went over to Jude and touched the girl's bare brown shoulder. "Are you okay?"

Jude was trembling. Her voice came out a ragged whisper. "No, I'm not okay. How can I be? I saw you burn the house. I *saw* it, Zibby, with my own eyes!"

Zibby walked over to the house, holding her breath, ignoring Jude's warning hand on her arm. She wanted to see if the nasty doll was there, too. And yes, sure enough, there she was. Back up in the nursery. The painted mouth looked smug. *I'm back,* she seemed to be saying. *You won't get rid of me so easily.*

Jude backed away from the house and headed over to Zibby's bedroom door.

*She's going to leave, of course,* thought Zibby. *She's going to leave me alone with this.*

But Zibby was wrong. Instead of leaving the room, Jude closed the bedroom door and came back to sit on Zibby's bed. "You must know something about this," she said, rubbing her hands over her arms as if to warm herself up. "That's why you were burning the house, right?"

Zibby walked over and checked the air-conditioning. It wasn't even on high. Jude's shivers came from fear, not temperature. Zibby turned her back on the dollhouse and sat next to Jude. She reached for her pillow and hugged it to her chest. "I'll tell you about it," she said. "I've been wanting to tell someone, but I didn't think anyone would believe me. It's too weird."

"I'll believe," said Jude, glancing over at the dollhouse.

"Let's go downstairs, then," said Zibby. "I want to get away from it — and her."

"Who?"

"Come on." Zibby jumped off the bed. "I'll tell you

downstairs. Outside. Over at your house. As far away as we can get. So she won't hear me."

With a troubled glance at the dollhouse, Jude followed Zibby out of the room.

The girls didn't talk much as they walked together down the street to Amy's house — *Jude and Penny's house,* Zibby reminded herself. They climbed the steps of a porch very much like Zibby's porch, but in much better condition, and full of healthy green plants and flower boxes.

"Now don't say anything till we get up to my room," Jude cautioned Zibby. "Try to act as though nothing's happened."

"Sure. Okay." Zibby marveled that her voice sounded so normal.

Inside, Jude led Zibby to the den, where Mrs. Jefferson and Penny were sitting on the couch looking at a magazine together. Unpacked boxes were stacked in one corner.

"Hi," Penny said in a subdued voice, throwing Zibby a hurt look. Obviously she was still upset about the dollhouse Zibby wouldn't sell her.

*If she only knew,* thought Zibby. And then thought, *Well, I'll tell her about it, too.* Penny might have some ideas that could help to deal with the problem of the dollhouse.

"Nana, this is Zibby from down the street," said Jude in a bright, cheerful voice. "Zibby, this is my grandmother, Claudia Jefferson. Penny's mom."

Zibby pushed the dollhouse from her mind and smiled at Mrs. Jefferson. "Hi," she said. "You don't really look like a grandmother." Then she flushed. "I mean — hello." Aunt Linnea always scolded her for making personal remarks to people.

But it was certainly true that Claudia Jefferson didn't fit the image of a white-haired, cookie-baking grandmother, wearing a starched apron and wire-rimmed spectacles. No, she was instead a tall, angular woman wearing loose white trousers and a baggy blue-and-white striped T-shirt. She had short, tightly curled black hair and smooth, unwrinkled deep brown skin. Only the creases around her eyes when she smiled showed the passing of the years. She smiled now at Zibby.

"Hello, dear. How nice for Penny and Jude that they've met you so soon. We were afraid they wouldn't know anyone until school starts."

"Yeah, it's nice for me, too," said Zibby. "My best friend Amy lived here — only a week ago. So I thought I wouldn't have anyone to do things with this summer, either."

"Oh, my, was the Cummings girl your friend?" Mrs. Jefferson looked sympathetic. "Moving is always harder on the kids than on the adults. And poor Jude has had to move twice recently — first from her house to ours, and now with us to this new house."

"I'll survive, don't worry," Jude said lightly. She glanced over at Zibby. "Um, Nana, we're going up to my room, okay?"

Penny closed the magazine she and her mother had been reading. Zibby noted the picture of a Victorian dollhouse on the cover and the title *Nutshell News.* Dollhouses again! There seemed to be no escape. "Me, too?"

Jude groaned, but Mrs. Jefferson nodded. "I'm sure Penny would enjoy Zibby's company, too, Jude dear." Then she smiled at Zibby. "We're very sorry it didn't work out that she could buy your dollhouse. Poor Penny was very disappointed. But I can understand your mother's not wanting you to sell it." She tapped the magazine with a manicured fingernail. "Some dollhouses are really worth a fortune. You'll want to keep yours as an heirloom, I suspect."

Jude made a choking sound, but Zibby spoke up quickly. "Yes, I'm really sorry. But I bet Penny can find an even better one." *Any* house would be a better one.

The three girls went up to Jude's bedroom. It was the one that had been Amy's little brother's room. The wallpaper had pictures of sailboats all over.

"Noddy says we can paint it and fix it up for me, but I haven't decided what I want to do with it," Jude said, seeing Zibby looking around. "Anyway, my dad and mom both love to sail. I sort of like the sailboats. It makes them seem closer." She pressed her lips together for a second, and Zibby realized for the first time that Jude must miss her parents a lot. It could not be easy to come to live with grandparents, even if you loved them, and then move again, leaving behind your school and friends as well.

"So." Penny clasped her arms around her knees and looked up at the other two girls expectantly. "What's the big secret?"

"How do you know —" began Zibby. "I mean, what makes you think there's a secret?"

"Oh, Penny always can tell these things somehow," said Jude with a sigh. "It's one of the many bizarre things about her. I can fill you in on some of her other peculiarities later. But I suppose we can tell her."

"That's what I was thinking, too," said Zibby. "We need all the help we can get on this."

"What?" asked Penny. "Something about the doll-house, right?"

Zibby regarded her in surprise. "Keep guessing," she said. "Maybe we won't have to tell you a thing after all."

"No, go on. I just guessed it was about the doll-house because it was so mean of you to promise it to me and then suddenly change your mind. You didn't seem like a naturally mean person — not like Jude for instance." This was said with a grin.

Jude swung out her leg and kicked Penny gently. Penny laughed. Zibby was beginning to see that the two girls really liked each other a lot under all their bickering and complaining. She wished she were as close to Charlotte as Jude was to Penny, but even before Charlotte changed into her new, ladylike self, she and Zibby had never been especially close. Charlotte was just too bossy. Uncle David liked to say, indulgently, that Charlotte had been born bossy. Zibby didn't think that was something he should smile about.

Zibby drew a deep breath now and exhaled loudly. "Okay. Listen to this and tell me what you think." Then she hesitated. "I'm not sure where to start."

"Where else but the beginning?" said Penny simply.

And Jude added, "Once upon a time . . ."

Zibby nodded. "Once upon a time," she began slowly. "It was my birthday. And I wanted to go to Sportsmart and buy new Rollerblades, but my mom dragged me along to Columbus — to a miniature show . . ."

Jude sat on the bed with her knees drawn up. She rested her chin on them, closing her eyes as she listened. Penny sprawled on the floor, her eyes wide and fixed on Zibby's face, fascinated. Zibby told them how she seemed to have been looking for the dollhouse even before she saw it. She told them about the bell and the stinging palms of her hands. She told them about how the nasty doll returned from the trash, and the dollhouse returned from the dump.

She was surprised that they accepted her account so readily. She herself would have probably been more skeptical. On the other hand, Penny believed in magic. And Jude had seen the burning house reappear, unburned, for herself.

When Zibby finished talking, Jude remained silent. But Penny jumped up. "This is so cool!" she said. "It's the kind of thing that happens in books! I can't believe it's true."

"Believe it," said Jude softly. "I saw the house in flames myself. And now it's back in Zibby's room, just the same as ever."

"But the thing is, what do I do now?" asked Zibby.

"You mean, what do *we* do?" Jude corrected her. "We're in this together — if you want us to be."

"It can be the reason for our club!" cried Penny in excitement. "We'll have a club to figure out what to do about the haunted dollhouse."

*The haunted dollhouse.* The words made Zibby feel chilled. But the girls' support warmed her again. "Thanks, you guys. I do want your help. I've already tried to get rid of the house, but it won't go. I want to get rid of the nasty doll, but she won't go, either. I don't know what else we can do."

"It's very weird the way the house comes back," said

Jude. "But I think what's even weirder is the way things you play in the dollhouse sort of come true — but in a bad way. Your cousin cracking her head on the bathtub after you dumped the doll baby in. Your mom burning her wrist after the mother doll's sleeve caught on fire during the blackout." She sat silently for a second. "But what if you could play *good* things, like having a genie or something? Maybe you could make anything you wanted to have happen really happen. Maybe you could make all your wishes come true, just by acting them out with the dolls!"

So far Zibby had been thinking only of how to get rid of the dollhouse. That she might accept whatever magic it offered and actually get it to work for her, had never entered her mind. But now she sat on Jude's bed, mulling it over. "I suppose we could try," she said slowly.

"Yeah!" shouted Penny. "Let's go over to your house and try right now."

"But what will we do? I mean, *how* will we try?" Zibby felt nervous about going back up to her room again.

"Well," said practical Jude. "Think of something you've wanted to have happen."

"I've wanted to go to Disney World," said Penny. "Let's play that the dolls go to Disney World and see what happens."

"No," objected Jude. "It's not your turn to wish, Penny. The dollhouse is Zibby's and she should have the first chance to test it out."

"Thanks," said Zibby wryly. "I'm not sure that's much of an honor." She sat thinking. She thought of her dad in Italy with the woman named Sofia. She thought of Amy far away in Cleveland, starting a new life in a new house with new friends. "Well," she said slowly. "I miss my dad a lot. But Italy's much farther away than Cleveland."

Jude and Penny just looked at her. Zibby realized they didn't know what she was talking about. "I've been missing my friend Amy like crazy," she told them. "She's really great. We could play that Amy comes back."

"Oh, right," said Jude dourly. "Great."

Zibby stared at her, not understanding the sarcastic tone.

"And are you going to play that we move back to Pennsylvania?" asked Penny in a small voice. "Because if you are, I don't know where we're going to live. We sold our house, you know, to move here."

And then Zibby understood. "Oh, no!" she told them. "I don't want you to move away! I'm really glad you came to Carroway." She realized it was true. But how could she bring Amy back if the Jeffersons were living in her house? "How about if we get Amy back here for a visit?"

Jude smiled. "Okay, but how will we know she wasn't just planning to come back anyway for a visit? I mean, how will we know if the dollhouse has the magic or not?"

"Amy and I begged and begged for her to be allowed to stay with me until school ended and then for a month of summer, and her parents said absolutely not," Zibby told her. "They said Amy *might* be able to come back during the winter vacation, but not before then. They think it's important for her to immerse herself in life in Cleveland before she can come back here — that's what they said, *immerse herself,* like it's a pool or something."

"Okay," said Jude.

"How long does it take for the house to make things work?" asked Penny.

Zibby considered. "So far it's happened almost right away. Within an hour."

"Perfect," said Jude, standing up. "Let's go try it now."

# Chapter 13

The girls knelt on the floor in front of Zibby's doll-house. Zibby ran her hands lightly over the roof, marveling at the smooth shingles — unmarred by the bonfire. She unlatched the front of the house and swung it open, revealing the rooms inside. Jude opened the pillowcase and shook the dolls out onto the carpet. Penny reached up in the attic for the frown-faced doll.

"No," cautioned Zibby. "Leave that one alone, Penny. That one is bad news."

Penny hastily replaced the doll back up in the doll-house attic.

Zibby took charge. "Okay," she said, lining the little dolls up on the floor in front of them. "Let's see. This one can be my mom. It's the doll that got burned." She picked up the doll in the blue dress and set her aside. "And this one can be me, because we have the same color hair." She selected a servant doll with red hair and laid it next to the mother doll.

"Now you need an Amy doll," said Jude. "Which one is she?"

Zibby considered the remaining dolls. "Well, this one with dark braids would do, because Amy has dark hair. But she doesn't have braids. She has short hair."

Jude shook her head. "How about this one?" She picked up a doll with short dark curls.

"That's a boy," objected Zibby. Then she shrugged. "But I guess it won't matter. I mean, I pretended the baby was Charlotte. It's what we play with the dolls that matters, right?"

"We'll soon find out," murmured Penny.

Zibby took up the mother doll and the Zibby doll and stood them in the kitchen. "Okay, here goes." She cleared her throat, then giggled. "I don't really know what to say."

"Just say what you really would say," advised Penny, and Jude agreed.

Zibby nodded. "'Mom,'" she whined, tipping the girl doll back and forth as she spoke. "'Mom, I miss Amy. I *need* to see her again. You *promised* I could invite Amy to visit!'"

"'Now, Zibby,'" she made the Nell doll answer, "'don't make such a fuss. You now how busy Amy must be getting settled in her new home. Her parents said she can come to visit in the winter. They want her to *immerse* herself in Cleveland before she comes back here.'"

"'Mom! Winter is ages and ages away!'" Zibby

walked the girl doll around the kitchen and stood her by a window. "'I can't wait that long.'"

"'Well, dear,'" said the mother doll. "'Maybe something will work out. It would be nice to see Amy again. I certainly don't mind if she comes to visit. It's just that I can't drive up all that way to Cleveland.'"

Zibby sat back and looked at Penny and Jude. "How am I doing?"

"So far so good," said Jude. "But I think you should play that Amy actually comes."

"I will," said Zibby. "I'm working up to it." She picked up the mother doll and made her speak. "'Listen, what's that? I hear a car pulling into our driveway.'"

"'This is amazing,'" cried the girl doll, running to the window. "'Come and look at this, Mom! You'll freak out. It's Amy's dad, and he's got Amy with him!'"

"'How amazing,'" said the mother doll. "'Let's go greet them.'"

Jude picked up the Amy doll. Penny reached for the father doll with the mustache. "This will be Amy's dad," she whispered.

Jude settled the dolls inside the Kleenex box on Zibby's night table, and slid it across the rug to the dollhouse. "Vvrrrroooom," she said. "This is the car, driving up." She and Penny each took a doll and marched them up to the front door.

"'Ding-dong!'" cried Jude. "'We're here, Zibby! It's Amy! Open the door!'"

Zibby moved the girl and mother doll into the hall-way and struggled to open the little door. Jude walked the father and Amy dolls into the house. "'Hooray! We got to come visit after all! And we're going to stay — how long should it be, Zibby? A month?'"

"Make it two weeks. That's more realistic."

"Okay." Jude tipped the dark-haired Amy doll as she spoke. "'We get to stay for two whole weeks, isn't that totally great?'"

Penny pushed the father doll forward. "'Yes, yes, isn't this wonderful,'" she said in a deep voice. "'I found I had a business trip to go on down this way, so I thought I'd bring Amy along.'"

"'That's totally super,'" said the Nell doll. "'— I mean, that's very nice indeed. Won't you come in and have dinner with us before you leave for your business trip?'"

"'No, thank you,'" answered the father doll. "'That's very nice of you to ask, but I must be leaving on my trip. Good-bye Amy. I know you'll have fun with Zibby.'"

"''Bye, Daddy,'" answered the Amy doll.

Penny marched the father doll out the door and back into the Kleenex box. Jude pushed the Amy doll inside with the Zibby doll and the mother doll, and pulled the little door shut.

Zibby sat back on her heels. "Okay," she said. "I guess that's it. Now we wait and see if anything really happens."

They heard a car pull up outside the house. Zibby raced to the window and peered out. Jude and Penny crowded close to see if Amy had arrived so soon. But the woman who got out of the car was the neighbor from across the street. The three girls watched as she walked up her path and into her house. They sighed.

Then the telephone rang.

The girls drew in their breath and stared at each other. Zibby jumped up and tiptoed out into the hallway. Downstairs she could hear the murmur of her mother's voice, then laughter. Zibby edged down the stairs, motioning for Jude and Penny to follow her.

"That will be wonderful," Nell was saying on the phone in the kitchen as Zibby, Jude, and Penny darted through the dining room and hovered in the kitchen doorway. "I'm sure the kids will have fun."

Zibby poked her elbow into Jude's side. *This is it!* Who would have believed the magic — or whatever it was — could work so fast? Maybe that old doll wasn't so nasty after all!

"So we'll see you all on Saturday night." Nell listened again, smiling. "Yes, it'll be nice — catching up after so many years."

*Years? What did that mean?* Zibby frowned. When Nell hung up, Zibby stepped into the room with Jude and Penny close behind.

Nell looked up. "Oh, hello, girls." She smiled at Penny. "You must be Jude's aunt."

Penny nodded shyly. "I'm Penny."

"That was Dr. Cummings, wasn't it, Mom?" Zibby hugged herself. "And he's bringing Amy to visit, right?"

"Wrong." Nell looked surprised. "That was Ned Shimizu — remember, we met him and his kids at the restaurant on your birthday? He's asked if we'd all like to go out for pizza together on Saturday. Why in the world do you think Dr. Cummings would be calling me?"

Zibby's shoulders slumped. "Never mind." She shook her head and left the room, the other two girls trailing behind.

"Oh, well," said Jude philosophically. "It was really just a wild guess, wasn't it, that the dollhouse might make some good magic, too."

"Yeah, I guess so," said Zibby. She led the way back to her room and flopped across the bed. The dollhouse sat as they'd left it, with the Amy doll being welcomed in the front hallway. The phone rang again, but this time none of the girls bothered to get excited. It would just be that Ned whatever-his-name-was, or Aunt Linnea, or somebody else for Nell.

But only a few minutes later, Nell appeared in the doorway of Zibby's room, a puzzled expression on her face. "Honey? That was Amy's dad on the phone just now. He said he has to go to a dental convention in Columbus, and can bring Amy along to visit you. He'll drop her off here tomorrow afternoon on his way.

She'll be able to stay for two days, and then he'll pick her up when he's driving home again." She came in and sat on the edge of Zibby's bed. "Of course I said we'd be delighted — but, Zibby, how did you know? Or had you already called Amy and arranged this with her?"

"I didn't *know,*" Zibby said. "And I didn't call Amy. I just — sort of hoped."

Jude and Penny carefully refrained from looking at each other. They stared over at the dollhouse, awed and a little frightened.

Nell was still frowning. "It's just very odd —"

She broke off as Zibby threw her arms around her in a hug. "Don't worry, Mom! It's just a coincidence."

Nell opened her mouth as if she were about to speak, then closed it and left the room. The three girls hugged each other in giddy excitement. Amy was coming! She would stay only two days instead of two weeks, but other than that, it seemed as if the dollhouse magic had worked perfectly.

Zibby woke up in the morning with excitement tingling from her toes up to her ears. She jumped out of bed and threw on her shorts and a T-shirt, then raced downstairs. Before she'd finished eating her cereal, Jude and Penny were knocking on the kitchen door.

Zibby let them in. The girls joined her at the kitchen table. Zibby reached for the plate of home-made donuts dusted with powdered sugar that Nell had made for a graduation breakfast she was catering this morning, and offered them to Jude and Penny. Penny took one and crammed it into her mouth.

"It's so cool!" Penny spoke with her mouth full, crumbs flying everywhere. "Just thinking how Amy will be here this afternoon kept me up all night! Brought by magic! Are you going to tell Amy, Zibby?"

"Sure, I'll tell her. But I'm not sure she'll believe me. She'll just say it was her dad's convention that brought her. Nothing like this ever happened to us before. It's like something that happens to kids in books, isn't it?" Zibby shook her head in amazement. She hadn't slept very well either. "It's just so weird to think we can — wow, Jude, think of this — we can do *anything*. We can play anything with the dolls and make stuff happen! Let's go upstairs right now and play something else. One of you can have the next turn. What will you wish for?"

Jude traced her finger along the table's edge. "I think we should be careful."

"What do you mean? We've figured it out now, and you've already seen that the magic works." Zibby wanted to run and shout out her excitement, and she didn't like the thoughtful look on Jude's face.

"I just mean — well, Amy isn't here yet."

"Come on, Jude," said Penny. "If you don't want your turn at the dollhouse, then let me have it."

Jude bit her full lower lip. "All right. I'll play next."

Zibby took her cereal bowl to the sink and rinsed it out, feeling virtuous. She even put away the donuts and wiped the sugar off the table with a sponge. Amy was coming and she wanted the house to look nice.

The girls went upstairs to the dollhouse. Zibby opened the house and Penny lined up the dolls on the rug. Then she took off her backpack and pulled out her own family of fat, long-haired trolls — mother, father, girl, boy, and baby. She added these to the parade on the rug. "When it's my turn," she said, "I'm going to check whether it's the house that's magic, or the dolls. I'm going to try with my trolls."

"Go ahead, choose your players," Zibby said to Jude. "Or do you want to try the trolls?"

Jude hesitated. "I'm not so sure I like this magic." She surveyed the dolls. "There aren't any black dolls. How can I play something about my family?"

"I don't have any black trolls, either," said Penny. "They should make some."

"They really should," said Jude. She sat staring at the dolls with a frown.

Zibby sat back on her heels and waited. Penny chewed on the end of one of her braids. Jude sat frowning at the dolls for another long moment, then sighed. "Well. Here goes." She selected the mother and father dolls, and stood them over by Zibby's bed. "These are my mom and dad, far away in Africa, working to set up hospitals in places that don't have any." Then she picked out the girl doll with the long brown braids and stood her inside the house. "This is me — even if it has only two braids." She tossed back her dozens of skinny braids with a clicking of beads. "We'll say the dollhouse is our new house here in Carroway."

"And these two servant dolls can be Penny's mom and dad," said Zibby, picking out two more dolls from the lineup. "And this girl doll can be Penny. Maybe it doesn't matter what the dolls look like. Maybe it's what you pretend that makes the magic work. We used a boy doll to be Amy, remember, and the magic worked just fine."

"Okay." Jude accepted the old-fashioned dolls and stood them around in the parlor. "Here we all are in the living room, just hanging out and watching TV, when suddenly there's a phone call."

"'Brrrrring!'" squealed Penny.

"Right. And so Nana answers it." Jude walked the Nana doll over to the table. "'Hello?' she says. And then she gets all excited. 'It's Mac! He's calling all the way from Africa!'" Jude reached over and stood the father doll up by the bed. "'Hi, Mama, it's me, Malcolm. We're just fine, but we're calling to say we're coming home earlier than we expected. We miss Jude.'"

"Hey, wait a minute," objected Penny. "Don't play that, Jude! I don't want you to leave. You're supposed to stay all year."

Jude's braids fell forward like a curtain shielding her face. "A year is too long."

"Oh, come on. Please don't play that they take you away!"

Jude shook her braids. "I thought you'd be happy to get rid of me, the way you act."

Penny picked at the rug. "Don't leave," she muttered.

Zibby intervened, picking up the Nana doll in the parlor and making her talk. "'Oh, Mac,'" she cried, "'it's wonderful to hear your voice. All the way from Africa, imagine that! But we don't want you to take Jude away. We want her to stay. Penny loves having her here, and so does her new friend, Zibby, who lives down the street!'"

Jude tossed back her braids and grinned. She tipped the Mac doll as she made him speak. "'All right, Mama. How about this for a plan? We miss Jude so much, we're going to make sure we come home for Christmas after all. We weren't planning to, I know, but we just can't be away from our darling girl for so long.'"

She picked up the mother doll, too, and pretended that she took the receiver from the father doll. "'Hello? I just wanted to speak to Jude for a second.'"

Penny picked up the Jude doll in the parlor and walked her over to the Nana doll. "I'll be you, Jude," she said. "'Hi, Sarah? I mean, Mom? It's me, Jude. I'm having a super time in Carroway. You don't need to come home at all.'"

"Wait a minute," objected Jude. "Let *me* do this." She reached into the house and grabbed the Jude doll. "'Mom? I'm glad you're having fun in Africa, and I'm fine here, but I miss you. I want you to come home for Christmas at least.'"

She made the mother and father doll answer from the bed. "'Okay, angel. We will.' There," she said, laying the dolls down on Zibby's bed. "That ought to do it."

"Now we just wait and see!" cried Penny. "Let's go to our house. They might be calling even now!" She bounced happily on the bed, and the little father and mother dolls plummeted onto the rug. She scooped them up and brought them over to the other dolls.

"Then let's get going," said Zibby. "I have to be back in time to meet Amy."

She and Penny started out of the bedroom. They stopped at the door.

Jude was still sitting on the floor by the dollhouse. She was looking at the spot on the rug where the mother and father dolls had fallen, a worried expression clouding her face.

"Coming, Jude?" asked Zibby.

Jude sighed and stood up. "Yes, I'm coming."

# Chapter 14

"Next time I should bring my toolbox," said Zibby, surveying the fallen tree in the Jeffersons' backyard. It was the one where Amy's tire swing had hung. Zibby pulled back some of the branches that rested on the ground and stepped between them. They formed a little room inside, leafy and green. "Hey, maybe we don't need to build anything," she called to the others. "Look inside here. It's a perfect little room already."

"We could have club meetings in here," said Penny.

"Until Noddy cuts it into firewood," said Jude, poking her head through the branches.

"A club to figure out what to do with the dollhouse," said Zibby. "I mean, we know there's magic — or something. But we need to plan what we want to use it for."

"We don't really know for sure that it will work," cautioned Jude. The girls had told Mrs. Jefferson to let them know if there were any important phone messages. From Africa, for instance. She had agreed, looking rather perplexed.

"It's awesome to think we can make anything happen," breathed Penny. "Anything!"

"It's a huge responsibility," said Jude softly, and the others looked at her, startled.

"What do you mean?" asked Penny, but Zibby thought she knew. She was just trying not to think about it because she wanted to keep the magic just for herself — and for her chosen friends. But if the dollhouse play would really make anything happen, then it was up to the girls not simply to use it for their own pleasure, wasn't it? Should they turn it over to grown-ups — to the government? They could use the dolls to play that world hunger was ended. Or that criminals never got away with any of their crimes. They could play that warring countries decided to stop fighting. They could bring about world peace.

Zibby had to smile, though, at the idea of the president bending over the dollhouse, moving the dolls around and playing.

But it could happen.

"We have to think of how we're going to use this magic," said Jude, and Zibby nodded.

"It'll be the Dollhouse Club!" said Penny. "With only us for members. Unless we decide to let other kids in. Right? And I want to be president, because it was my idea for a club."

"But it's my dollhouse," said Zibby.

Mrs. Jefferson appeared at the back door and Zibby's heart pounded. Had the call from Africa come already? But no, she was only asking them if Zibby would like to stay for lunch. Zibby decided she had better go home and clean up her room for Amy's arrival. She made Jude and Penny promise to call her as soon as they heard anything. So they left the leafy room without having settled anything more about the club.

"Is Amy here yet, Mom?" Zibby asked as soon as she got home. Nell was in the kitchen filling salmon cream puffs. Trays of mini quiches and delicate cheese straws covered the countertops.

"Not yet, honey. I wouldn't expect them till after two o'clock." Nell stopped her work to set a cheese sandwich and a bowl of fresh sliced peaches on the table for Zibby. She poured out two glasses of milk, then called into the living room for Charlotte to join them for lunch.

"What's she doing here?" asked Zibby in surprise.

"Aunt Linnea had to take Owen to the orthodontist, and she didn't want to leave Charlotte alone at home because she's still feeling dizzy."

Charlotte limped slowly into the kitchen. She was still uncommonly pale, but her superior expression was firmly in place.

"How are you feeling?" Zibby asked, looking at the bandage on Charlotte's forehead.

"Terrible," snapped Charlotte. She sat down and frowned at her food. "I don't like cheese sandwiches. Cheese makes you fat."

"I can make you a salad if you'd prefer it," said Nell mildly.

"I don't like salads," Charlotte replied grumpily, but she sat down at the table and began picking at her sandwich. Zibby ignored her, and ate her own sandwich in a distracted way, glancing out the window when she heard a car pass, sure that Amy had arrived.

After eating half her cheese sandwich and eating a sliced peach, Charlotte returned sulkily to lie on the couch in the living room. Zibby came into the room and sat in the armchair by the window, watching for Amy out the front window. The two girls didn't speak. Charlotte leafed through a fashion magazine she had brought with her, but after only a few minutes it dropped out of her hand onto the floor, and she was asleep.

Waiting, waiting. Waiting and waiting. Zibby picked up the magazine and turned the pages. She tried to read, but it all seemed so stupid to her. Hairdos and "The Coolest Clothes for Summer." Who cared? Skinny models with big smiles and windblown hair posed on beaches and in forests. Some were perched in trees. Zibby thought about how she and Amy used to climb the tree in Amy's backyard. Now that tree had fallen, and Zibby would be making a clubhouse with Jude and Penny. Things kept changing, and Zibby wasn't at all sure she liked it. She missed Amy. But at least Penny and Jude were nice.

Two o'clock came and went. Then three o'clock. The phone rang, and Zibby nearly broke her ankle in her rush to answer it, but it was only Jude, asking whether Amy had arrived. "Nothing," Zibby reported. "No sign of them. I'm going crazy."

"We haven't had any phone calls either," Jude said. "I'm going crazy, too." She laughed shortly. "And of course Penny's been crazy for years already, so there's nothing new with her."

Zibby hung up and went to the kitchen. She helped her mom make pear pizzettes topped with Brie cheese for a reception she was catering the next day. Charlotte woke up just as Aunt Linnea and Owen arrived to take her home.

Four o'clock, then five o'clock came, and finally Nell agreed that Zibby could call Amy's house to ask her mother what time Amy and Dr. Cummings had left. But there was no answer. Zibby left a message on the answering machine, feeling frustrated, then hung up and sat there, her hand tight on the receiver. What was she supposed to do now? Just sit waiting all night? Maybe they'd gotten the day wrong. Maybe they were coming *tomorrow* instead.

She gave a shriek when the phone rang under her hand. Taking a deep breath, she lifted the receiver. "Hello?"

"Zibby, is that you, dear? This is Jill Cummings."

"Mrs. Cummings! I just called you! They haven't arrived yet, and I've been waiting all afternoon. We did say today, didn't we? I expected them hours and hours ago."

"Zibby dear, I'm afraid I have bad news."

Zibby froze. "What bad news?" she whispered. Her mother came into the kitchen and stood listening, a frown creasing her smooth forehead.

"There was an accident on the way, and the car is completely totaled. Both Amy and her dad were knocked out and taken to the hospital."

"Oh, no!" Zibby's stomach churned with fear.

"They seem to be fine now, just shaken, as you can imagine." Mrs. Cummings gave a worried little laugh. "And they have big bumps on their heads. They both have to stay overnight for observation, and John won't be able to walk for some time —"

"John?" Zibby repeated stupidly. She could hardly hear what Amy's mother was saying over the bell clanging in her head.

"Yes, I'm afraid Dr. Cummings has a badly broken leg."

"Oh, I'm so sorry." Zibby bit her lip. Nell came over and placed a hand on her shoulder.

"We're all sorry, dear. But we're lucky no one was killed. Still, I'm afraid this means there won't be a visit for you girls any time soon."

Nell reached for the phone, so Zibby mumbled good-bye and handed her the receiver. The two mothers started talking, but Zibby wandered away, not wanting to hear. She climbed the stairs to her bedroom, her legs moving as slowly as if she were walking underwater. She rubbed her hands together, trying to lessen the stinging in her palms.

She sank onto her bed and stared over at the dollhouse. The dolls she had left lined up on the rug were scattered about the room, and the nasty doll was out of her box. She was perched on the dollhouse roof, her unpleasant expression surveying the bedroom.

Zibby didn't bother to remove the doll. She didn't even want to touch her — it. Was it the doll's fault that Amy and her father had been in a terrible accident? Or was it her own fault, for trying to make them come to her in the first place? She put her hands over her ears, but the bell in her head kept ringing.

Nell entered the room and came to sit next to her on the bed. "I'm sorry, honey," she said, hugging her. "But it's amazing their injuries weren't worse. They swerved off the road and hit a tree head-on."

"What — what made them swerve?" Zibby made herself ask. "It isn't raining or anything."

"It's very odd. Dr. Cummings says he swerved to

avoid a woman who darted suddenly across the road directly into the path of their car. A woman in a gray dress."

Zibby's eyes darted to the dollhouse roof, then back to her mother. "Did they hit her?"

"No. And there was no sign of her after the crash."

Dinner that night was a subdued affair, with Zibby thoughtful and sad, and with Nell simply quiet, resting her bandaged hand on the table as they ate a simple meal of soup and salad. If Amy had been there, they would have ordered out for pizza and made ice-cream sundaes for dessert to celebrate. But now there was nothing to celebrate.

That night before going to bed, Zibby gathered up all the dolls and put them away in their pillowcase. She picked up the nasty doll off the roof, holding her at arm's length. She dropped her into the wastebasket by her desk, knowing full well the doll was unlikely to stay there. When she went to bed, sleep didn't come for a long time. She remembered she hadn't called Jude and Penny, but it was too late to call now. Tomorrow she would call them, and Amy, too. The pillow felt lumpy. She could see the full moon outside her window, glowing like an empty face. And when sleep finally came, it was fitful.

She tossed and turned under her sheet. Her dreams were filled with dolls, and a flickering woman in gray, darting across roads into darkness. In the morning she woke up thinking about Jude's parents, far away in Africa.

Nell came into the room, dressed for work. "There's a phone call for you, honey. Take it in my room, then hurry down to breakfast. I'm leaving in ten minutes."

Zibby dragged herself out of bed and across the hall to her mom's room, almost afraid to take the call. "Hello?" she said, her voice groggy.

"Oh, Zibby!" It was Jude, and after this greeting she broke into tears.

"Oh, no, what is it? What is it, Jude?" But Zibby was afraid, horribly afraid, that she already knew.

"Don't play with the dollhouse anymore. Don't even touch it!" More sobs, rising hysterically, and then Penny's voice came on the line.

"Zibby? Something bad has happened. We just got news from Africa."

"Wh-what happened?" Zibby almost didn't dare to ask. Her palms were stinging again, and the bell that had grown quiet in her head began ringing softly.

Penny's voice sounded awed. "Mac and Sarah fell off a cliff. In Kenya. They were hiking with friends. Sarah — that's Jude mom — is all scraped, and bruised, and has a broken hand. But at least she'll be okay. But Mac — there's no sign of him. They think he fell into the river and has been washed away. Sarah called just a while ago with the bad news. Zibby, Mac might be dead!"

Zibby closed her eyes, remembering how the father and mother dolls had fallen off the bed.

"Oh, Zibby," Penny cried. "Was it our fault?"

"I don't know," whispered Zibby. She glanced over at her mom, who was regarding her curiously. "I hope not."

"I've got to go. We're all out of our minds here. But we had to tell you. And to ask how things are going with Amy."

"It's not going." And, quickly, Zibby told Penny about the accident.

There was silence on the other end of the line when she finished.

"What do we do now?" pressed Zibby. "We have to do something."

"I don't know," sighed Penny. "Look, let's get together now, in our clubhouse."

"All right. I'll be over right after breakfast."

"No one feels like eating in our house." Penny's voice was sad. "Oh, Zibby, how can we ever eat again, if Mac is really dead?"

"I — I don't know," whispered Zibby. "I just don't know."

# Chapter 15

Just as Zibby was leaving the house, Aunt Linnea drove up and dropped Charlotte off. She had errands to do in Columbus, and had arranged with Nell that Charlotte would come over. "I just don't want her left alone at home," she said. "Not with her head still aching so badly."

Nell was off with her trays of food to cater a reception after a golf tournament at the Carroway Country Club. She kissed Zibby and Charlotte good-bye, and told them to take good care of each other. Charlotte slumped on the couch, staring at the morning talk show on TV and muttered an unhappy-sounding good-bye. Zibby hoped Charlotte would just stay home, but Charlotte asked where Zibby was going, and then insisted she was coming along.

"But your head," protested Zibby.

"I'm sick of lying around," snapped Charlotte.

"There is no reason why I couldn't have just stayed at my house. My mom is so dumb."

Zibby hesitated. She didn't want Charlotte being bossy and rude to Penny and Jude, especially now when they were so scared and worried. But Charlotte was determined to come.

As they walked down the street, slowly because of Charlotte's headache, Zibby filled Charlotte in on the bad news about Amy and about Jude's dad. She didn't mention the dollhouse. There was no point. Charlotte would think magic was something only babies believed in.

Zibby walked ahead of Charlotte, leading the way to the Jeffersons' backyard. She pushed through the leafy branches of the fallen tree and found Penny and Jude sitting inside the clearing. The branches overhead made a green roof. The low branches made benches. Summer sunlight filtered into this bower and made it look peaceful. But the girls inside were clearly feeling anything but peaceful. Their eyes were puffy; their cheeks were stained with the tracks of tears. Zibby sat next to Jude on a branch and bumped shoulders.

"Hi," she said softly.

Jude smiled wanly. Then she and Penny saw Charlotte peering through the branches. "Um, my cousin wanted to come over, too," Zibby explained. "This is Charlotte."

"I know," said Penny.

"Are you the cousin who bashed her head on the bathtub?" asked Jude. And when Charlotte nodded, fingering the bandage on her forehead, Jude turned to Zibby. "See? That's another accident that's the dollhouse's fault."

Charlotte looked puzzled. Then she ducked under the branch and came into the little room. With her hand, she brushed off invisible specks of dirt from the branch before sitting down on it. "What do you mean about the dollhouse?"

"Haven't you told her anything?" Jude asked Zibby.

Zibby shook her head. She wished Jude hadn't mentioned the dollhouse. She tried to change the subject. "About your dad," she said. "I'm really, really sorry."

"Well you should be," mumbled Jude. "It was *your* evil dollhouse —"

"Jude!" cried Penny. "That's not fair and you know it."

Jude dipped her head, her braids falling forward to hide her face. "No, you're right, of course it's not Zibby's fault. Not really. Maybe my mom and dad would have gone on that same hike whether we played with the house or not. Maybe they would have stopped to help the woman they thought was hurt anyway —"

"Woman? What woman?" asked Zibby.

"A woman my mom said they heard calling for help."

Zibby took a deep breath. "Was she wearing a gray dress?" she asked, her mouth dry.

Jude looked at her sharply. "How should I know? All I know is, they heard a woman calling to them for help, but they didn't find anyone. And then they fell."

"Why didn't we notice before?" moaned Penny. "It seemed at first that whatever you played with the dolls came true, but it doesn't come true exactly as you play it. It comes true with something gone horribly wrong."

"We don't know for sure," began Zibby — then stopped, glancing over at Charlotte.

"Know what?" asked Charlotte, guardedly.

Penny glanced at Zibby. "You should be the one to tell. It's *your* dollhouse."

"I wish it *weren't* mine," said Zibby fiercely. "You know I've tried to get rid of it. But if I can't give the thing away or throw it away — or even burn it up — then what am I supposed to do?"

"Burn it?" yelped Charlotte. She grabbed a fistful of leaves and stripped them off the branch. "Why would you want to burn up your beautiful dollhouse? Stop being such a child, Zibby. Even if you don't like the house, it's a collector's item. It's not just something you can throw out! Give it to me if you don't want it."

Zibby looked at Charlotte squarely. "I don't think I could give it to you even if I wanted to. It wouldn't stay with you."

Charlotte tossed her hair. "You are so silly with your childish games, Zibby Thorne. When will you grow up?"

"It's hardly a game when people are getting hurt," snapped Zibby. Then she sighed. "All right. But if we tell you, you have to promise to keep it a secret."

"Oh, sure," said Charlotte airily.

"No, really," pressed Zibby. "You have to promise not to blab about it to your friends. This is private. And you have to promise to try to help us figure out what to do."

Despite herself, Charlotte looked intrigued. "Okay, okay, I promise. Scout's honor."

So Zibby reluctantly told her about the dollhouse and the dolls, and about the tests they'd made. Penny and Jude chimed in with details.

"Well," said Charlotte when they'd finished. "That is *quite* a story. I'm surprised you haven't called the newspaper to report it yet."

"I knew you wouldn't believe us," said Zibby shortly. "Fine. Then just sit there and shut up while we try to figure out how to get rid of it."

"Whoever sold it to you sure had a lot of nerve," muttered Jude. "Whoever owned this dollhouse must have known perfectly well that it was bad news."

"It was at the miniature show," Charlotte said. "It was a bargain because it was so dirty."

"Yeah," snorted Penny. "I'll bet. I'm surprised they didn't just try to *give* it away!"

"An old woman sold it to me," Zibby said.

"Well how come she was able to sell the house?" wondered Penny. "I mean, why didn't it just keep on returning to her? You know, like she sold it to you, then went home and found the house back up in her bedroom — just like what's been happening to you?"

"I don't know," admitted Zibby. "Maybe it wasn't magic for her. Just for me."

"But why should it just be magic for you?" demanded Jude.

Penny shook back her braids with new determination. "Look, I'm going to go crazy if I just sit here waiting to hear about Mac. Let's *do* something. How about if we find this woman and take the house back to her. And try to get your money back, Zibby."

"The receipt said no refunds."

"And the miniature show was in Columbus only for that one day," said Charlotte. "It's not a store you can just go back to."

"Still, we should try," Penny maintained. "Do you know the woman's name, Zibby?"

"No," admitted Zibby. "But there must be a way to track her down."

"Maybe my mom knows. I could ask her," Charlotte offered, to Zibby's surprise.

They stayed outside under the fallen tree talking until Charlotte complained that she felt dizzy again. "I'm going home," she murmured. Zibby stood up and brushed off her shorts.

"No," said Charlotte. "You stay here. I want to go home to *my* house. It just kills me that my mom is being so unreasonable. I'm not a baby. What does she think's going to happen?"

Zibby shrugged. "Still, I think you'd better come back to my house." She said good-bye to Penny and Jude, and followed Charlotte. She was glad Charlotte didn't insist on going to her own house, and was even more glad when they got back to Zibby's house and Charlotte collapsed on the couch with her eyes closed.

"You just rest," Zibby said. "I'll make lunch."

"I don't want anything," snapped Charlotte. "Just let me lie here."

Zibby left the room and went to the kitchen. She slapped together a peanut butter and blueberry jam sandwich, grabbed a plum from the bowl on the kitchen counter and went up to her bedroom. She switched on the air conditioner and sank onto her bed.

She felt tired and anxious and wished as much as Charlotte did that Charlotte could go home to her own house. She didn't feel like having anyone else around, but wanted to put her head down on her pillow and sleep until Jude's dad was found safe and sound.

She lay back on her bed and closed her eyes, exhausted. The uneasy nights were quickly catching up with her. The thrum of the air conditioner and the humidity pressing outside the windows made the room seem to be whirling. She closed her eyes. Maybe she dozed. All she knew is that when she next opened them, she saw Charlotte kneeling on the floor in front of the open dollhouse.

"Hey!" Zibby struggled to sit up. "Don't mess with it. I don't want any more trouble."

"Oh, come on," scoffed Charlotte. "You don't *really* believe what you were saying with Jude and Penny, do you? Sometimes you're so incredibly childish, I can't believe we're related."

"Just leave the house alone!"

"Okay, don't freak out. I'm just looking at the dolls."

But she wasn't just looking. She was moving them around and murmuring. "What are you doing?" Zibby demanded. "I told you —"

"Relax, it's just a game." Charlotte laughed over her shoulder. "How about this, Zibby? I'm playing that this is my house, and I'm left alone one night while my parents are out. This blonde-haired girl doll is me. And then robbers come — see? These two servant dolls are the robbers. And I'm not scared at all. I catch them in the act and tie them up with — let's see, with what? I packed away all my old jump ropes. But an electric cord would work, too." She reached up and pulled the ribbon off her ponytail. "See? The electric cord. Now, I'll just tie them up and call the police." She shook back her long blonde curls, then tied up the dolls and laid them on the dollhouse parlor floor. "Okay, and then my parents return. And they're totally amazed at how responsible I am, and decide they'll never have to worry about leaving me home alone ever again." She smiled over her shoulder at Zibby. "The end."

Zibby sat on her bed, angry at Charlotte but without the energy it would take to argue with her. She watched Charlotte remove all the dolls from the house, then start stacking the furnishings on the floor next to them. "This house is so filthy," Charlotte said. "Let's clean it up, Zibby. It could actually be really nice, you know. I have some extra wallpaper at home from when I papered the upstairs of my dollhouse. I could let you have it. I bet there's enough to do the front hallway. But we should do the outside of the house first."

Zibby remained on her bed, unmoved, as Charlotte ran to the bathroom and came back with a wet washcloth. She didn't offer to help as her cousin started scrubbing the roof of the porch, rubbing the grime of years off the shingles and pillars. "If you cleaned this house up, you'd like it a lot better," Charlotte said. "Look how much nicer it is already."

She went back and forth to the bathroom, washing

out the dirty cloth, scrubbing the roof and the clapboard siding, then polishing the little glass windows.

Zibby watched in stony silence.

She only joined her cousin in front of the dollhouse when Charlotte cried out in pleasure. "Look, Zibby! The house has a name. Did you see this?"

Zibby looked where Charlotte pointed, at the small brass plaque, green with age, fastened just below the peak of the roof on the front of the house. She hadn't noticed it before because it had been hidden under layers of grime.

"Primrose Cottage," she read. "That's a pretty name for such a nasty house."

"You're impossible, Zibby." Charlotte frowned, and seemed about to say something else, when both girls heard the door opening downstairs, and Nell and Aunt Linnea's voices.

Zibby jumped up. "I'm going to ask if they know the old woman," she said. "Don't you say anything about why I want to know. Remember your promise — Scout's honor and everything."

Charlotte rolled her eyes. "But I'm not really a scout, Zib."

"Still, you promised!"

"I'm pleased that you're interested enough in the dollhouse to want to trace its history," Aunt Linnea said. "But the miniature dealers who come to the convention are from all around the state, and even from other states. I recall the woman who sold you the house, but I'm afraid I never saw her before."

Zibby sighed. She should have known it wouldn't be easy.

Aunt Linnea looked thoughtful. "I know that a lot of the houses that were on display in Columbus came from Lilliput, a shop over in Fennel Grove. Why don't you call the shopowner — her name is Lydia Howell. Ask whether she knows the woman you're looking for. Possibly she works for Mrs. Howell, helps in the shop, you know."

"She looked pretty old to be working," Charlotte put in suddenly. "She was a mass of wrinkles, like one of those funny hairless dogs. She must be a hundred years old."

"Charlotte, that's not kind," said Aunt Linnea firmly.

"Well, thanks," said Zibby. "I'm going to call that shop and ask."

Aunt Linnea smiled. "I have to go over to Fennel Grove tomorrow. If Charlotte is feeling well enough, I can take you along and drop you off at Lilliput. It's a fascinating shop, so you'll have fun looking around even if Mrs. Howell doesn't have any information about the woman who sold you the dollhouse. How about it?"

"Perfect!" Zibby hugged Aunt Linnea. "And may I

ask my friends, Penny and Jude, to come along? They're really interested in dollhouses, too."

"The more the merrier," said Aunt Linnea. "That's why we drive a van."

She and Charlotte said good-bye, and drove off. Zibby phoned Amy to ask how she was feeling after the accident. Amy sounded depressed, and worried about her father, who was still in the hospital. She didn't know when — if ever — they'd make it for a visit back to Carroway. *Probably never, the way things are going,* thought Zibby, but she tried to sound optimistic while talking to her friend. After she'd said good-bye to Amy, she phoned Jude to ask whether there had been any news about her dad. There hadn't, Jude reported, sounding even more depressed than Amy had. Zibby changed the subject — *though it's all really the same subject, after all,* she thought — and told Jude about Aunt Linnea's invitation to the miniature shop in Fennel Grove the next morning. Jude said she and Penny would love to come, and she sounded more cheerful by the time they hung up.

The phone rang a short time later while Zibby was helping Nell wash the empty food trays from the morning's reception. Nell answered, then gasped. Zibby turned off the water. She saw her mom gripping the phone tightly. "Oh, no," said Nell. "Oh, that's terrible. What a blessing no one was home at the time! Have you called the police? Is there anything I can do?"

Zibby rushed to her side. "Mom, what's wrong?" *What has the dollhouse done now?*

After another moment, Nell hung up. She ran her fingers through her hair. "That was Linnea," she said. "They'd only just arrived home, when they saw something had happened. The front door was open — the lock had been shot out."

"*Shot* out?"

"Someone broke in while Linnea was gone and Charlotte was here with you. The thief stole a lot of valuable stuff and trashed the rest of the house. David's art collection, Owen's music equipment, a lot of Linnea's most precious miniatures — all gone or ruined. Who would do such a thing?" Nell shook her head disbelievingly. "Here in Carroway? I can hardly believe it."

Zibby shivered, remembering the game Charlotte had played with the dollhouse dolls. Here was more doll-play come true — and again gone badly wrong.

"The only consolation," Nell was saying, "is that Linnea hadn't left Charlotte home alone. After all, the thief had a gun. I don't even want to think about what might have happened if he'd found her there."

"He?" asked Zibby. "Do the police know it was a man?"

"Well, no," admitted Nell. "There's no evidence

pointing to anyone, I'm afraid. Aunt Linnea said all the police detectives could find when they searched the house was a scrap of gray cloth caught on a snag of wood by the front door."

Zibby went back up to her room. She felt chilled despite the warmth of the day. She crossed the room to switch off the air conditioner — and stopped. The nasty doll was perched on the windowsill, her long gray skirt spread neatly around her. And then Zibby noticed something she hadn't seen before. There was a tear in the skirt, with a small piece of the fabric missing entirely.

# Chapter 16

Charlotte lived on the other side of Main Street, where all the homes were large and old, built by the first families to settle in Carroway. The streets were named after spices. Large trees shaded the sidewalks. Zibby, Penny, and Jude rode their bikes under a green canopy of leaves past Coriander, Sage, and Thyme, then turned onto Nutmeg. Zibby led the way up the driveway of Charlotte's big brick house and braked to a stop. "Here we are."

Penny and Jude dismounted and left their bikes in the driveway with Zibby's. They followed her up to the front door. Zibby reached for the doorknob, and found the door locked. She rang the bell and waited.

After a moment Charlotte opened the door. "Hi," she said, and her voice was subdued. The large bandage that had been on her forehead since the accident had been replaced by a much smaller one that just covered the stitches.

"You don't usually lock the door," observed Zibby. "But I guess we'll all have to lock up now if there are burglars in town."

"I guess." Charlotte stood aside to let them inside. "Come on in. Mom's almost ready."

"I'm surprised your mom still feels like taking us to Fennel Grove," said Zibby.

Aunt Linnea came into the wide center hall and smiled wanly at the girls. "Oh, but now I need to go to Fennel Grove more than ever. I need to stock up on cleaning supplies."

"Zibby told us the burglars trashed your house," said Penny.

"Did they ever!" Aunt Linnea laughed shortly, but it didn't sound as if she found anything funny. "You must be the new girls in town. Well, come right on in and see the carnage. I hope this won't give you a bad impression of Carroway — we've never had problems with crime before."

"This is Jude and Penny Jefferson," Zibby said, remembering that her aunt hadn't met her friends. "They live in Amy's house now." And to the girls she added, perhaps unnecessarily, "This is my Aunt Linnea."

"How is poor Amy?" asked Aunt Linnea. "Nell told me about the accident."

"I called her last night, and she said she's okay. Her dad is still in traction, though, with his broken leg."

"And what about your dad?" Charlotte asked Jude. "Has he been found yet?"

Aunt Linnea raised her eyebrows, and so Zibby hastily explained about the accident in Kenya. Jude bit her lip. Penny shook her head. "No news," she said quietly.

Aunt Linnea shook her head. "It seems we're having a spell of bad luck around here, doesn't it?" Then she went to get her purse.

Charlotte led the girls into the living room, and Zibby gasped at the sight of the usually orderly room. Books had been hurled to the floor, the potted plants lay on their sides, spilling dirt on the carpet, the furniture was askew, the curtains had been ripped. They walked through the dining room, family room, and kitchen, all of whose contents seemed to be lying broken or marred on the floors. Charlotte stopped by the door to the basement.

"Now for the worst of all," she said. "My poor new dollhouse has been murdered."

"Oh, no," said Zibby, hardly able to look.

Aunt Linnea's basement workroom was a fascinating place to Zibby, usually full of woodworking tools and a wonderful smell of sawdust and paint. But today the sight of the workroom made Zibby cringe. Balsa wood littered the floor. Paint had been spattered on the walls and over the dollhouse Aunt Linnea had been working on.

The dollhouse sat on the floor next to her worktable. It wasn't as large as Zibby's dollhouse, but it was clean and neat and brightly painted with lavender paint. The little front windows had newly built, white-painted window boxes filled with tiny silk flowers. The roof had been splintered by a heavy blow from an ax.

Charlotte turned her back on the mess and faced the other girls. "You guys were right. It *was* the dollhouse," she said in a low voice. "It must be because I played that robbers game yesterday, Zibby. Oh, Zibby, you were right. It's true."

Zibby knew this was no small concession coming from her cousin. She didn't feel like gloating, though. The wreckage all around them made her sad — and angry. She and Charlotte quickly explained to Jude and Penny about the game Charlotte had acted out in Zibby's dollhouse the day before. Then Aunt Linnea called them upstairs to leave for Fennel Grove. They piled into the van and rode to the next town in silence.

When they had pulled up in front of the miniature shop, Aunt Linnea turned in her seat and smiled at the girls. "Who can tell me where that name comes from?" She pointed to the wooden sign in the shape of a house hanging over the front of the shop.

*Lilliput.*

Zibby didn't have the faintest idea. "Isn't it the name of the owner? Mrs. Lilliput Howell?"

"Some kind of flower?" guessed Charlotte.

"Yeah," agreed Penny. "You know, like a lily that you put somewhere. Lily-put."

Aunt Linnea was shaking her head.

"It's from *Gulliver's Travels.*" Jude's voice held a faint note of superiority. "You know, the book about the guy who travels all around, and gets captured on some island by some really tiny people. Lilliputians. They tie him up with rope."

"Cool," said Penny. "Little people? Was it a real island? With little live dolls?"

Aunt Linnea laughed at her. "They were real people, not dolls. Of course, there's no such thing. And no such thing as live dolls, either."

Zibby, Charlotte, Jude, and Penny exchanged a glance, but didn't say a word.

Aunt Linnea told them to tell Mrs. Howell she would come in to say hello when she finished with the shopping and the bank. The girls would have about an hour on their own.

Zibby led the way inside, followed by Charlotte, Jude, and Penny. All four of them stood silently just inside the door, looking around in amazement.

The shop was full of dollhouses. Of course Zibby had seen a lot of dollhouses at the miniature show, but here the effect was almost overwhelming. The shop interior looked like a whole neighborhood built for tiny people. There were huge Victorian houses with towers, the rooms open to view, and houses like her own, with fronts that swung open when you wanted to play, but stayed closed and latched when you didn't. There were townhouses and farmhouses and even a schoolhouse. There were shadowbox rooms, single rooms decorated to be on display. A hat shop, a bakery, a hardware store. Most of the houses were empty, but the ones in the window and the ones in the center were decorated beautifully. Other houses were in various stages of construction. Zibby looked carefully at the dovetailed joints on one of the unfinished houses with approval. Somebody was a good carpenter. She wondered whether Mrs. Howell did her own work or hired other people.

The answer came almost at once as Mrs. Howell ducked out from behind the purple-and-blue-striped curtain at the back of the shop. She was wearing a carpenter's apron like Zibby's with many pockets. The pockets bulged with nails.

"Why, hello, Charlotte dear," said Mrs. Howell, beaming at them over the sales counter. "You look more like your mother every time I see you. How nice you could come by, and bring your friends. I'm always eager to meet fellow miniaturists."

Looking self-important, Charlotte introduced the other girls. Mrs. Howell beamed at them each in turn.

"Now you girls feel free to look around. Maybe you'll get some ideas for decorating your own dollhouses. Just holler if you need anything. I'll be in the back room."

"Mother says to tell you hello," remembered Charlotte. "And she'll be back for us after she finishes her errands. We did want to look around but mostly we wanted to talk to you."

"Oh?"

"Zibby bought a house at the miniature show the other week," Charlotte explained.

"You bought a house from me?" Mrs. Howell looked puzzled. "How funny that I don't remember you, dear. Which house was it?"

Zibby glanced at the other girls. "I didn't actually buy the house from you. But Aunt Linnea said you might know the woman who did sell it to me. I need to find her. I want to, um, give her the house back again — if I can."

Mrs. Howell looked surprised. "Give it back?"

Zibby looked at Jude for help. Jude looked at Penny. Penny shrugged. Charlotte fiddled with a miniature bed on the counter.

"Now, girls, what's this all about?" pressed Mrs. Howell.

"Well, I want to buy Rollerblades instead," Zibby said. That, at least, was both honest and something Mrs. Howell might be able to believe. "Aunt Linnea thought you might know who the woman was. She was very, very old, with white hair." She realized this description would fit thousands of senior citizens, but didn't remember anything more identifying — except for her intensity, and the expression of relief on her face when Zibby said she wanted to buy the house.

Mrs. Howell frowned, thinking. "Well, I may know the woman you mean, but it was more than a year ago that she came to me and said she wanted me to have her dollhouse. Wanted me to sell it for her. I told her I built my own houses and didn't take others in to sell. Then she said she'd *give* me the house. She didn't want the money — she said she was moving into a nursing home and couldn't take the dollhouse with her. She just wanted the house to go to some nice child. So I agreed — it *was* a lovely house, or it could have been if it were cleaned and repaired. I told her I'd take it, and she drove it over one afternoon. We put it in the back room so I could fix it up. But then the next morning when I came in to work, it was gone."

"Gone," repeated Zibby, nudging Jude.

"Just like —" began Jude, then stopped.

Mrs. Howell nodded. "I knew it must have been stolen, yet nothing else in the shop was disturbed, and the door had been locked when I entered. I was very puzzled, and I still am, actually. I wanted to call the woman to tell her what had happened, but she hadn't left me her phone number. I wasn't looking forward to calling every Parson in the phone book, but then I remembered she said she was moving into a nursing home. There's only one in Fennel Grove. It's called Fennel Hills. So I called there — and found her. And, can you believe it? When I told her I was afraid the dollhouse had been stolen, she told me not to worry about it."

"Then that must mean that whoever stole it sold it to you, Zibby," said Jude, a puzzled frown creasing her forehead.

Mrs. Howell shook her head. "No, the person selling the house at the miniature show was quite definitely Mrs. Smith herself. I was shocked when I saw her there with the house. But when I confronted her, and asked her how she came to have the house if it had been stolen, she just looked vague and mumbled something about bad pennies always turning up." Mrs. Howell shrugged. "Perhaps she stole it back herself. Though why she would do that, I don't know. And how she managed it, with the door locked, I can't imagine. All I can say is, there was something strange about the whole business."

Then the doorbell jangled and a young woman walked in holding a little girl by the hand.

"Excuse me, girls," Mrs. Howell said, and walked over to the newcomers.

"Fennel Hills," Jude whispered to Zibby. "That's where we'll find her."

"I wish Aunt Linnea would hurry up," Zibby whispered back. "We're hot on the trail!"

"I know she's probably too young," the customer began in a soft, pleasant voice after Mrs. Howell had greeted her. "She's only three. But I can't wait to get her set up with a dollhouse. I think every girl needs a dollhouse to play with and decorate and love."

"I couldn't agree more," said Mrs. Howell with a smile for the child. "Girls and boys both."

"I still have the one my grandfather made," the young mother continued. "It was my mother's and then my sister's and mine, and we decorated it exquisitely. I'll pass it down to Jenny when she's old enough. But for now, a good sturdy dollhouse for her little stuffed mice is what we need."

"Mouse house," piped up Jenny.

"Yes, sweetheart." Her mother laughed. "And we'll make a little sign for it and attach it to the front door. 'Jenny's Mouse House.' How would you like that?"

"Mouse house!" Jenny chortled gleefully, and Penny, Jude, and Charlotte laughed along with her. Only Zibby stood silent, staring at the little girl. She remembered the little brass plaque Charlotte had discovered when she was cleaning the front of the dollhouse. A wild thought had occurred to her.

Mrs. Howell and Jenny's mother had turned to the simple wooden dollhouses and were talking together in low voices. "What was Mrs. Smith's first name?"

Zibby asked abruptly, not even bothering to excuse herself for interrupting.

Mrs. Howell looked up. "Why, I'm not sure I ever knew it, dear. No, wait a minute. She did say, after all. It was a flower name, a nice old-fashioned name. Pansy? No, that isn't it. Petunia? No . . ."

Charlotte jostled Zibby's elbow in excitement.

"Was it *Primrose,* Mrs. Howell?" Zibby squealed.

"Why, yes, dear! That's it. But however could you know?"

Zibby explained about the name inscribed on the front wall of the dollhouse. Mrs. Howell had never noticed it under all the dust and grime.

Then Aunt Linnea's van pulled up outside the shop. The girls thanked Mrs. Howell for her time, and left her still in deep conversation with Jenny and her mother about the perfect home for a family of mice.

Zibby and Charlotte begged Aunt Linnea to take them straight to the Fennel Hills nursing home, but she said she had to get home. Repairmen were coming to the house to repair the broken windows and replace the shattered mirrors. She might be able to take them the next day. Zibby swallowed her disappointment. Then she had the idea that they could ask Nell to drive them back to the nursing home. When Aunt Linnea pulled into Zibby's driveway, Zibby asked, "How about if Charlotte stays for a while?" If Nell would drive, they could leave right away.

"No, I'm afraid not," said Aunt Linnea. "Charlotte is going to be helping me at home."

"Oh, Mom!" wailed Charlotte, but Aunt Linnea remained firm.

Zibby, Jude, and Penny said good-bye and went into Zibby's house. Nell was coming down the steps wearing a fresh, flower-sprigged sundress and white sandals instead of her usual shorts and T-shirt.

"Mom," began Zibby. "Will you please drive us to Fennel Grove right now? We want —"

Nell cut her off with a smile. "Sorry, honey. Not now. Ned and I are going out for dinner together. We had at first planned to bring you children along — you and his two, I mean — but decided that on our first date, it would be better to go alone."

"First *date?*" squealed Zibby, all thoughts of Primrose Parson momentarily forgotten.

"Dinner date," said Nell. "A simple dinner date."

Aunt Linnea leaned out the window of the van and grinned at her sister. "A date!" she cried. "That's great, Nell."

Zibby scowled. It couldn't be a *date.* Dad might still come back to live with them some day. . . . *What, bringing Sofia along?* Zibby tried to push the reasonable inner voice aside. Anything might happen. Her dad could change his mind. What if she played with the dollhouse dolls that her dad divorced Sofia, said it was all a mistake, and returned home to live with them again? Could it work? Could she bring him back to them by magic?

*But think how badly the dollhouse messed up everything else.* The voice of her conscience stabbed at her. What if her dad and the unknown Sofia had a car accident or fell off a cliff and died, or something else horrible? She knew very well she couldn't trust the dollhouse.

She waved good-bye to Aunt Linnea and Charlotte, then sank down onto the steps of the front porch. Jude and Penny hovered nearby.

Nell put her hand on Zibby's shoulder. "How about if Jude and Penny stay for dinner?" she suggested. "I've got lasagna waiting in the oven for you. And there's a salad. Everything's ready."

Zibby perked up. "Want to?" she asked the other girls.

Jude and Penny glanced at each other with troubled eyes. "We would love to," began Jude, "except —"

"We need to go home," finished Penny. "See if there's been any news yet —"

"From Kenya," added Jude. "You know."

Zibby nodded. She felt bad that in the excitement of tracking down Primrose Parson, she'd forgotten for a short time how worried the Jefferson family was. "We'll do it soon. As soon as we have some good news."

"I'm sure that will come soon," said Nell optimistically. Then she headed back upstairs. "Well, Zibby, I'll see you later. We'll be home by dark. I've invited Ned to come back with me for dessert and coffee."

"A *date,*" muttered Zibby. "I can't believe it."

"Aw, forget it," said Jude. "Listen, I've got an idea. Let's just phone Primrose Parson at the nursing home! We don't have to talk about everything on the phone, but at least we can make a date —"

"A *date!*" said Penny with a little grin.

"Make an *appointment* to see her as soon as we can get someone to drive us. Aunt Linnea said tomorrow might work, and that would be good because Charlotte could come, too." Zibby was surprised at herself for even wanting to include her cousin, but since Charlotte had become involved with the dollhouse mystery, she hadn't been acting quite as prim and snooty as usual.

"It's not really so far to Fennel Grove, anyway," said Penny. "I bet we could bike there if Charlotte's mom won't take us. Normally I'd ask my mom, but she won't want to leave in case there's word from Mac . . ."

Zibby nodded, pushing her mom's date with Ned Shimizu to the back of her mind. When Nell came downstairs again, perfume wafting around her, Zibby hugged her good-bye.

Before they left, Penny and Jude sat down with the phone book and looked up the Fennel Hills nursing home. Zibby dialed.

"Fennel Hills," announced a cheerful male voice on the other end of the line. "How may I help you?"

"Um, I'd like to speak with Mrs. Smith," Zibby said. "Primrose Smith."

There was a silence, then the sound of a throat being cleared. "*Ahem*! Are you by chance a relative of hers?"

"No —" said Zibby, wondering whether she should say she was.

"Oh, too bad," said the man. "We have been trying to trace her relatives since she was transferred."

"Transferred?" Zibby was confused. Her dad's job transfer had taken him to Italy. How would they ever find Primrose Parson if she had gone to Italy?

"Transferred to the hospital," the man on the phone was explaining. "I'm afraid she had a bad heart attack a few days ago."

"Oh, no!" Zibby said, and twisted the phone cord around her hand tightly. Jude and Penny stood by looking puzzled.

"Yes, I'm sorry to say it's true. Perhaps you can reach her at the hospital."

"Which hospital?" asked Zibby, and Penny and Jude groaned.

"Highland Hospital, right here in town," he answered. Zibby thanked him and hung up.

After Zibby told Jude and Penny, Jude grabbed the phone book. "Want me to call?"

Zibby shook her head. "She sold the dollhouse to me. I'd better talk to her."

Zibby reached a nurse who told her that Mrs. Smith was out of her room having tests done, and could not speak on the phone. But visiting hours began the next morning at ten o'clock. Zibby asked whether she could leave a message for Mrs. Smith.

"Certainly," said the nurse.

"Tell her I'm the girl she sold her dollhouse to. Tell her that — tell her that I want her to take the house back."

"Take it back?" asked the nurse in surprise.

"Yes," Zibby replied firmly. "Because there's something — terribly wrong with it."

"Now, now," laughed the nurse. "What could be wrong with a dollhouse?"

Zibby glanced over at the solemn faces of her friends. She saw the ache in their eyes as they worried about Mac. She thought of Charlotte at home, cleaning up her ruined house.

"It's . . . *evil,*" said Zibby. "That's what."

# Chapter 17

## *Primrose (1919)*

"'You're evil, and you deserve to be fed to the dogs,'" said Primrose Parson gleefully, speaking for the little girl doll. She and the other children had tied up the governess and were stuffing her into a closet. "'Now just sit here until we make sure the dogs are hungry enough.'" Primrose laid the dolls on the dollhouse schoolroom floor and ran to her bedroom for the stuffed dog she kept in her bed. He was worn and limp — she'd slept with him since she was a baby younger than the little twins. But since her other toy animals had been left in the nursery with Nanny Shanks, old Fred would have to do. She carried him back to the dollhouse, checking, as she passed, that Miss Honeywell's bedroom door was still closed.

Miss Honeywell had ended Primrose's lessons an hour early today because she felt she was coming down with a sore throat. She sent for the kitchen maid to bring her some hot tea with lemon and retired to her room to rest. Primrose was delighted with the extra playtime, especially as she had been having some wonderful games with the dollhouse dolls lately.

She had created a whole family, and servants, too. The dollhouse parents traveled a lot — not as much as her own real parents, but still they traveled. Primrose had a hard time imagining parents who stayed home all the time. And when the parents were gone, the dollhouse children were in the care of the governess, Miss Sourpuss. Primrose made Miss Sourpuss act every bit as nasty as the real Miss Honeywell, but unlike Primrose, the dollhouse children managed to find fitting punishments for their governess every time she stepped out of line. Primrose could only dream of such vengeance against Miss Honeywell, but she had fun planning the punishments. In fact, torturing the governess doll had become her favorite game. It wasn't as satisfying as playing real practical jokes on the real governess, of course, but at least she didn't get her hands smacked or get herself locked in the closet.

Primrose tiptoed past Miss Honeywell's closed door and then hurried back to the dollhouse with Fred. "Here is Fred," she said, stuffing the dog into the dollhouse schoolroom. "He's the most ferocious creature this side of the Atlantic. His chief pleasure is eating mean people. Go ahead, Fred — enjoy yourself!" And then she acted out how Miss Sourpuss ran around trying to escape the huge, dripping fangs of Fred, and how the children laughed when she was finally chomped to little, bloody bits.

But then Primrose realized that if Old Sourpuss were dead, the children wouldn't have anyone else to punish. So she played that Old Sourpuss — evil thing that she was — came back from the dead, more menacing than ever. She tried to lock all the children into the closet, but they attacked her and overpowered her. Then they bundled *her* into the closet! The dollhouse didn't really have a closet, so Primrose just used the little box the governess doll had come in. Stood on end in the corner of the dollhouse room it made a perfect prison.

Miss Honeywell's scratchy throat turned into bronchitis, and she was ill for almost two whole weeks. Primrose had a wonderful time. Out from under the governess's watchful, repressive eye, she was able to run into the nursery wing whenever she wanted. She played with Poppy and Basil and went with them and Nanny Shanks to the park. She ate her meals with them in the sunny playroom. And then, after lunch, she rocked one of the babies while Nanny Shanks rocked the other. They sang lullabies together until the little twins fell asleep in their arms. And then, when the twins were laid snuggly into their cribs for a nap, Nanny Shanks and Primrose had time for games of checkers and pick-up sticks, just as they'd used to play together. Primrose was so busy with Nanny Shanks and Basil and Poppy, she didn't have time to play with the dollhouse.

But then Miss Honeywell recovered. She ordered Primrose back to the schoolroom and heaped work upon her, "to make up for lost time," as she said. So while Nanny Shanks and the babies were out in the fresh air making snowmen, Primrose sat at her table and memorized lists of spelling words. While Nanny Shanks sang and played, Miss Honeywell scolded and shouted. While Nanny Shanks cuddled, Miss Honeywell smacked, declaring that Primrose was the most unmannerly and ill-behaved child she had ever seen.

Primrose turned to her dollhouse again with a sense of desperation. *There,* at least, the governess was put in her place. *There* the governess was punished. She played that the doll children pushed the governess doll out the windows, stuffed her down the chimney, hanged her from the ceiling. She felt some measure of relief in this play, but the real Miss Honeywell still loomed large and horrible.

One afternoon in December after lessons had ended — and Primrose had been smacked twice for not being able to locate China on the world map fast enough to please her governess, who accused her of laziness and indifference — Primrose turned to the dollhouse for solace. Miss Honeywell left the schoolroom on some errand of her own, and at last it seemed the air was clear again, and clean to breathe. Primrose always felt choked around her governess, never knowing when her anger and disapproval would be roused.

Primrose took the mother and father dolls, who had been traveling over by the wardrobe in her bedroom, and set them on the back of her stuffed dog. "Here come the parents, galloping home on their horse," she murmured. "They want to be home in time for Christmas. They've brought so many presents home for the children, even Santa Claus would have a hard time bringing more." Her own mama and papa would be home for Christmas, too. It was the one bright star that had kept her spirits up since their last visit.

"And just as the parents arrive home from their trip, Old Sourpuss is upstairs taking a tonic for her sore throat. It has been bothering her for a long time, and the children hate the sound of her *hack, hack, hack.* It keeps them awake at night, even worse than her snoring." Primrose picked up the two littlest dolls and made them speak.

"'James the gardener made the mice in the walls be quiet by giving them some of this special powder in their mouse hole,' the tiny girl doll said. 'Maybe it would help to quiet Old Sourpuss's cough, what do you think?'" And then the boy doll answered: "'What a fine idea! Let's ask big sister to help.'"

Primrose marched the girl doll into the dollhouse schoolroom. "'Why, what a wonderful idea. You are such smart children!'" The doll children tipped the whole box of Rodent Killer into Old Sourpuss's medicine bottle. Then Primrose moved the taller governess doll in the gray dress into the room. "'*Hack, hack, hack,*'" she coughed for the governess doll. "'I shall need another dose of tonic. And after that I will punish the children again since they didn't know where China was on the map today.'"

The governess doll swallowed a large spoonful of tonic. Then another. "'My oh my, this tastes even more delicious than usual —'" Primrose made the doll stagger around the dollhouse attic. "'But, oh my, I feel so dizzy and short of breath. And — oh, no! I feel the most dreadful, painful cramps! *Hack, hack, hack!* Help, I can't breathe!'" The governess doll tumbled to the floor. Primrose grinned as she moved the doll children over to her.

"'I'm afraid she's dead,'" said the boy doll.

"'Nothing to be afraid of,'" answered the sister doll. "'Not anymore.'" Primrose smiled with satisfaction. "And now they have to get ready for the funeral. The parents arrive just in time." She turned from the house to get the parent dolls, and drew her breath in sharply.

There stood Miss Honeywell, right behind her. She had entered the schoolroom and walked across the room to the dollhouse without making a sound. And

Primrose, so engrossed in her play, had not noticed. Miss Honeywell had been listening. She had seen and heard everything.

The skin on Miss Honeywell's face looked tight, and her eyes glittered with a dangerous light. "Killing off the governess, eh?" she said in a low, hard voice. "Killing me off, were you?"

"N-no! Miss Honeywell, it wasn't you — of course not!"

The smack caught Primrose hard across the cheek and knocked her backward. She crashed into the dollhouse, then quickly regained her balance and turned to run away. But Miss Honeywell had her now, tight in an iron grip. "Into the closet with you, my girl. Into the closet now — and out you'll come tomorrow morning and not a moment before."

All night in the closet! "No!" cried Primrose.

She kicked and screamed for Nanny Shanks, but Miss Honeywell dragged her to the closet and slammed the door. "Please let me out, Miss Honeywell," begged Primrose. "Please!"

Primrose heard the key grate in the lock. "That's *Sweet* Miss Honeywell to you," came the reply, and then the *tap-tap* of Miss Honeywell's firm footsteps — moving away.

Primrose sank down into the darkness of the closet and pressed her fist to her mouth. All night! How would she bear it, here in the dark, in the cold, all alone? She huddled on the floor, pressed into the corner.

She cried until she could cry no more, and her breath came in soft gasps. The crack of light under the door faded to a deep gold, and Primrose knew the sun was setting. Her stomach felt hollow, but there would be no dinner. She told herself to be strong, to be a soldier. She wouldn't let *Sweet* Miss Honeywell win.

She must have dozed because when she next opened her eyes, the crack of light under the door was gone. She heard footsteps on the wooden floor and Miss Honeywell's harsh voice: "Primrose? I hope you are thinking about your behavior. Such a sinful game. Your parents, when they hear, will be deeply shocked. I hope you are properly ashamed of yourself."

Primrose did not answer.

"Are you, young miss? Are you ashamed?"

Primrose pressed her lips together and did not say a word. Let Miss Honeywell open the door to see if she were properly ashamed — and then she'd dart past her so fast Miss Honeywell would be caught off balance and crash to the floor, breaking her neck! And Primrose would run and run and run . . .

But Miss Honeywell did not open the door to check on Primrose. All she did was stand outside the door and rant on about how ungovernable Primrose was. There *never* was a more undisciplined child. She must learn proper manners and good behavior for her own sake. And Primrose felt tears course down her face again because she knew her escape was just a fantasy. The door was thick. It was locked. It was going to stay locked because Miss Honeywell was not going to open it, and because Primrose didn't have the key.

Primrose put her hands to her ears to block out the governess's hateful rasp. Her fingers touched something hard. Her hairpins!

Primrose's long hair was braided into two plaits and then pinned up into loops behind each ear. She pulled at the pins eagerly now, and held them in her hands tightly. Hard, thin, long enough to fit into the lock — maybe she could escape from the closet after all!

After Miss Honeywell had finished scolding Primrose, she rattled the doorknob twice for emphasis. "I'll be back for you in the morning, young miss. And not a moment before."

Primrose waited until she heard the *click-clack* of Miss Honeywell's footsteps across the floor and was sure the governess had gone downstairs for dinner. Then Primrose set to work.

She poked the end of the hairpin into the lock and moved it up and down, pressed it all around. She tried the door handle — but no, the door was still locked. She tried the other one, jiggling it back and forth. But again, the door stayed locked. Primrose did not give up hope. She had tools, and she had time, and she would stay here at the door all night if she must, trying to pick the lock. Thieves did it all the time, that she knew from tales Nanny Shanks had told her. Patience, patience, that was all she needed.

If nothing else, trying to pick the lock gave Primrose something to do, and the hours in the dark closet passed very slowly indeed.

After a long while, when Primrose had grown quite discouraged, she had the idea to use both pins at once. She held them together and pressed them into the lock. At first nothing happened, but she felt a stronger resistance — something more to push against. She pushed the pins up and down, then rotated them, tightly held together, slowly in the lock. And then she half-heard, half-felt the tiny *tock* as the lock opened. Holding her breath, Primrose opened the closet door and stepped out into the schoolroom. She exhaled slowly and looked around.

The room was dark. The doors to her bedroom and Miss Honeywell's bedroom stood open; that meant Miss Honeywell was still downstairs. That meant there was still time, if she acted quickly, for a really good practical joke. This was one that Miss Honeywell wouldn't forget in a hurry!

Primrose sidled into Miss Honeywell's bedroom and went straight over to the dresser. On top of the dresser stood the large china bowl and pitcher full of water for washing. The third floor didn't have bathrooms, so both she and the governess had to wash and brush their teeth from the water in their pitchers, changed daily by the maids. For bathing they used the big bathroom downstairs. Next to the china bowl and pitcher was Miss Honeywell's ring of keys. Primrose picked it up and slid the closet key off the ring. She put it in her pocket.

Then Primrose lifted Miss Honeywell's pitcher. It was nearly full. *Perfect!*

She ran back to the schoolroom for one of the chairs, and carried it into Miss Honeywell's room. She stood on it, but couldn't reach . . . so she jumped down and looked around for what could be used to lift her even higher. *Aha! Miss Honeywell's night table!*

As fast as she could, Primrose cleared the lamp and Bible from the night table and dragged it over to the chair by the door. She stopped and listened, but heard no sounds from downstairs. Nonetheless, she must be quick or Miss Honeywell would return before she could get everything ready. And then it would be the closet again — this time probably for the rest of her life.

Primrose smiled grimly to herself as she heaved the table up onto the chair. It wasn't very heavy, but it wasn't very stable, either. She would have to be very careful, or she'd fall and ruin everything, and the trick would be on her.

Once the table was stacked on top of the chair,

Primrose clambered up, cautiously hanging onto the door for support. Yes, she could reach the top of the door. But — *oh, no, silly me* — she had left the pitcher back down on the dresser.

So she had to go down again and get it. Climbing back up again holding the heavy pitcher was not easy. In fact, several times Primrose nearly dropped the pitcher. Water sloshed out everywhere — all over her clothes and onto the floor. But at last she had the pitcher where she wanted it. Balanced right on top of the door.

The slightest movement would dislodge it, sending it pouring water all over whoever touched the door. That was the plan. *Whoosh!* Miss Honeywell would get the surprise of her life when she came up to go to bed.

But first of all Primrose had to get down from her tower without detonating her surprise. She held her breath as she considered how to climb off the night table and chair without jostling the door. Finally she decided just to jump, and leaped from her makeshift ladder right onto the middle of the governess's bed. The night table wobbled up on the chair, but it didn't touch the door, and the pitcher of water remained upright on its precarious perch.

*Success!* thought Primrose, grinning with relief. She quickly went about smoothing out the bedcovers, returning the night table to its place by the bed, and placing the lamp and Bible carefully where she'd found them. Then she carried the chair back to the schoolroom.

She had just pushed the chair neatly into place, when she heard the telltale tapping of Miss Honeywell's shoes on the stairs. She darted toward her bedroom to hide, then froze. No — not there. The safest place to wait and watch her practical joke would be the closet. She would lock the door again from the inside for extra protection. Miss Honeywell would get her ring of keys and not find the one for the closet, but she wouldn't be able to prove Primrose had taken it. Primrose raised herself on tiptoe and tucked the key high on the closet shelf inside one of the books. She grinned in the dark at the thought of a dripping-wet Miss Honeywell yelling at her through the door, dearly wanting to blame her for the soaking. "But, Sweet Miss Honeywell," Primrose planned to say. "Here I was, locked up in the closet all the time. How could I have done anything?" She stifled a giggle. And then she would beg to be let out, but Miss Honeywell wouldn't be able to find the key. She'd have to call one of the menservants to take the door off. And then everyone would know how cruel she was to poor Primrose.

Miss Honeywell's shoes *tap-tapped* into the schoolroom. Primrose waited, forcing herself to breathe deeply and evenly. But Miss Honeywell didn't come near the closet. The footsteps headed straight for her bedroom. Primrose jumped up, listening. Then she reached up and retrieved the key. She unlocked the closet door soundlessly and opened the door just a crack. She didn't want to miss out on seeing Old Sourpuss get soaked.

Miss Honeywell put out a hand to push open her bedroom door. She took a single step into the room, and at the same time the heavy pitcher of water — the entire china pitcher, not just the water — fell straight down onto her head with a solid thunk, raining water all around. Primrose watched from the closet with round wide eyes as the governess crumpled onto the floor atop thc shattered china.

It had worked even better than Primrose could have hoped. *Old Sourpuss will be plenty wet and bruised now,* thought Primrose with satisfaction. She waited for her governess to jump up and come to find her. "What's wrong, Sweet Miss Honeywell?" she would say in her most innocent voice. "Why do I hear water dripping out there?" She laughed under her breath at the wonderful satisfaction of this joke, her best practical joke ever.

But Miss Honeywell didn't jump up. She didn't move at all.

After a moment, Primrose opened the door a little wider. "Miss Honeywell?" she called.

No answer. Could the governess have been knocked unconscious?

Primrose edged out of the closet, her heart beginning to pound. Miss Honeywell was lying just inside the doorway, with her legs twisted oddly.

One look at Miss Honeywell's open glassy eyes and ashen skin confirmed an even more horrible truth.

*No,* thought Primrose. *No, it can't be. I didn't mean —*

As Primrose started screaming for Nanny Shanks at the top of her lungs, she heard, quite distinctly, Miss Honeywell's voice inside her head.

*"You did this to me, you vicious, unmannered brat! But I'll get you back, mark my words. I'll have my revenge, young miss — if it's the last thing I do!"*

# Chapter 18

In the morning after breakfast, Zibby rode her bike over to the Jeffersons' house. She found herself thinking of it that way now — the Jeffersons' house. No longer Amy's house. It had a different feel to it now that a new family had moved in.

She and Jude and Penny were going to ride to Charlotte's, and then on to the hospital to see Primrose Parson. No adult was able to drive them, but as Penny had pointed out, the hospital wasn't too far away. The parents all agreed that they could go by bike as long as they stayed on the bike paths. Highland Hospital lay along the main road between Carroway and Fennel Grove. They wouldn't encounter much traffic and could easily be there by the time visiting hours started.

Mrs. Jefferson came to the door looking haggard and sad. Zibby knew there still had been no word of her son in Kenya. Mr. Jefferson — Jude's grandfather and Penny's dad — greeted Zibby solemnly. He was glad, he said, that Jude and Penny had found a friend so soon after moving to Carroway. "Being with you helps take their mind off Mac," he added, patting Zibby on the shoulder as he moved past her into the living room. He heaved a sigh and sank onto the couch. Jude and Penny came downstairs then, and the girls said good-bye and left the house.

"Poor Dad," said Penny. "He's so distracted about Mac, he can't even go to work."

Zibby shook her head in sympathy. Jude mounted her bike in silence and set off down the road ahead of them. Zibby supposed Jude was as upset — or more upset — than Mr. Jefferson. It seemed to Zibby that while everyone in the Jefferson family was missing Mac, the loss of a father was even worse for Jude than the loss of a brother was for Penny, or of a son for Mr. and Mrs. Jefferson. Zibby felt glad suddenly that her own dad was safe and well — even if he was far away in Italy and married to Sofia.

They picked up Charlotte and continued on their way. The ride took about a half hour. Even though it was still morning, the summer sun beat down hot and heavy. Charlotte lifted her heavy blonde curls off her neck. For once Zibby didn't envy her. All the girls were sweating, though, by the time they biked to a stop in front of the big hospital.

*At last, at last, at last,* thought Zibby, leading the way

in the front door and over to the reception desk. She asked the silver-haired nurse sitting there where they would find Mrs. Primrose Smith.

The nurse consulted a sheaf of papers. "Ah," she said slowly. "Are you her grandchildren?" She glanced up at them. "Any of you?"

"None of us," said Jude firmly. "But we've come to see Mrs. Smith on urgent business."

"Urgent?" The nurse peered at them over her wire-rimmed glasses.

"Yes," said Penny eagerly, smiling her brightest smile at the nurse. "It's about her childhood dollhouse."

The nurse shook her head. "I'm afraid she won't be able to see you. She was moved to intensive care last night."

"But we talked to her on the phone just last night and she said she wanted to see us this morning." Zibby looked pointedly at her watch. "And visiting hours start right now."

"You must have spoken to her before she took a turn for the worse, my dear." The nurse pursed her lips. "Only family members are allowed to see patients in intensive care."

"But she doesn't have any family!" cried Penny.

"Would you *please* just check whether she wants to see us?" pressed Zibby.

"If she says no, we'll go away," promised Jude. "But if she says yes . . ."

"We won't upset her or make any noise," added Charlotte in her prim way.

The nurse frowned, then sighed. She picked up the phone on her desk. "All right, I'll check with the head nurse in intensive care."

The girls waited impatiently while the nurse talked on the phone. "Some children here to see Mrs. Smith — about a dollhouse. Is she awake? Will you ask her — ?" The nurse listened. Then, with raised eyebrows, she said good-bye and hung up.

"Well, it seems Mrs. Smith has been badgering the head nurse to allow you children to see her. So you may go up." She shook her head disapprovingly. "It's highly irregular, however. Be sure to check in at the nurses' station first."

The girls rode up to the intensive care ward in the gleaming elevator. Doctors and nurses got on and off at the different floors. People in green jumpsuits pushed important-looking carts of surgical instruments covered with plastic down the hallways. The girls followed the signs to the intensive care ward, then hesitated at a circular counter in the middle of the hallway.

"Is this the nurses' station?" Zibby asked tentatively.

"Yes, it is," answered the nurse on duty. "And you must be the young ladies to see Mrs. Smith. Come right this way." She set off down the hallway, then stopped in front of a closed door. As she opened it, she looked back at them over her shoulder. "Mrs. Smith wants to see you, but she's very weak — her heart has been giving her some problems lately. Usually patients on this floor are visited only by family members, but Mrs. Smith seems to be all alone in the world, and I thought it wouldn't hurt to let her see you."

"What's the point in living," came a querulous voice from the single hospital bed inside, "if you can't see people or do things? It's boring just lying here helpless all the time."

"I believe I'd feel the same way, Mrs. Smith," said the nurse in a soothing voice, leading the girls over to the bed.

And there lay the woman from the miniature convention, at last. Her white hair frizzed out from her head like dandelion fluff. Her blue eyes were very bright. "Ah, yes," she said, peering at Zibby. "You're the little girl who bought the dollhouse."

"I'm Zibby Thorne," Zibby said. "Isabel — that's my real name. And this is my cousin, Charlotte Wheeler. And my friends, Jude and Penny Jefferson."

"But we're not sisters," Penny piped up. "I'm her *aunt*."

Jude elbowed Penny. Charlotte stepped forward with adult poise. She held out her hand. "How do you do, Mrs. Smith."

Mrs. Smith laughed and then the laugh turned to a cough. The nurse hurried to her side, and when Mrs. Smith finished coughing, the nurse helped her lie back on her pillows again. The old woman was pale.

"Are you sure you're up to having visitors?" pressed the nurse.

"Yes, yes, I'm fine," muttered Mrs. Smith. "Now, you leave me to my company."

"Well —" the nurse hesitated. "All right." She showed the girls a button at the side of Mrs. Smith's pillow. "Buzz me if you need me." Then she left the room and closed the door.

The four girls pulled up chairs and sat in a row across from Mrs. Smith's bed. Mrs. Smith fingered the folds of her white hospital sheet. Her voice when she spoke was breathless and light, but the words came out fast, as if she couldn't hold them back. "All right, girls. What do you want to ask me? It's about the dollhouse, of course. I know that. But what has been happening? You must tell me. Oh, I *was* clever, wasn't I! My brilliant inspiration! And it worked — at last! Hasn't it?" She frowned at Zibby. "You *do* still have the dollhouse, don't you?"

"Yes," Zibby said. "I can't seem to get rid of it." She watched Mrs. Smith carefully to see if that would sound surprising to her.

But it didn't. Mrs. Smith just smiled. "Yes, yes! Ha-ha-ha! At last."

Zibby stared at her in astonishment, then felt the pressure of Jude's hand on her arm. "Yes, well, um, we've come because I want you to take the house back. I don't want it anymore."

The old woman smirked, her wrinkled face creasing with what looked to Zibby like mischief. "No refunds, no returns. It was the contract you signed, my dear."

"I know. I'm not asking for my money back, even. I just don't want the house. It's doing horrible things, I think. It's an evil house. And I think you know it!"

Mrs. Smith was shaking her head wearily. "Ah, no, dear. The house isn't evil. If anyone's evil, it's Sweet Miss Honeywell."

"Who?" asked Penny.

"Miss Honeywell?" asked Charlotte.

Zibby and Jude glanced at each other. "Is Miss Honeywell the doll?" Zibby ventured. "The nasty doll?"

"Well, not exactly," answered Mrs. Smith, and again her voice held that breathy, weary note. "No, Miss Honeywell is only *using* the doll, I think. It has become her body, you see, since she doesn't have one anymore."

The back of Zibby's neck prickled. "No body?" she asked. "What do you mean?"

Mrs. Smith just sat there, fingers plucking at her sheet, a rather unpleasant little smile playing at the corners of her mouth. "You have a ghost in your dollhouse, my dear."

Jude spoke up impatiently. "Really, Mrs. Smith, I think you owe it to us to explain what you know about the dollhouse. It's frightening us, and causing trouble —"

"What kind of trouble?" asked Mrs. Smith, leaning forward intently.

Charlotte fingered the edges of the bandage covering her stitches. "Well, people getting hurt, for instance. And robbers wrecking my house."

"Car accidents," said Penny. "And burns on wrists."

"And falls off cliffs," cried Jude. "My father might be dead because of the dollhouse!"

Mrs. Smith looked impressed. "My goodness. Sweet Miss Honeywell must be feeling very powerful indeed. But that's where you've gone wrong. Given her too much power."

"I don't understand any of this," cried Zibby. "What are you talking about?"

"All right," Mrs. Smith said. "I will tell you everything. But first let's be clear on one point even before I begin, girls. I will *never* take that dollhouse back. Do you understand me?" She peered at Zibby, blue eyes hard. "It's yours. You bought it. You signed a legal contract. I've rid myself of Miss Honeywell — I've outfoxed her at last, and I'm not taking her back!"

Zibby shivered. Mrs. Smith looked harmless enough, but her breathless voice had a cold strength behind it. Zibby decided she didn't like Mrs. Smith very much, even if she *was* old and sick. "All right," she agreed. "I won't try to make you take the house back if you promise to tell us the whole story. But will you at least try to help us get rid of it some way?"

"Shall we burn it?" laughed Mrs. Smith, breaking off in a coughing fit. She lay back on her pillows and tried to bring herself back under control. Then she struggled to sit up. She peered at Zibby with knowing eyes. "Chop it up with an axe? Drop it into the ocean off a boat? Oh, yes, dearie, don't look surprised. I've tried all that and more. Nothing works, as I think you know."

"But *why?*" demanded Penny. "Why does the house come back?"

"Miss Honeywell makes it." And suddenly the spark was going from Mrs. Smith's voice and she was just an old, sick woman again. She slumped back against the pillows. "Miss Honeywell is haunting it. She was my governess. My parents were gone a lot, traveling, visiting friends, who knows? They never took us children along. We stayed home with the servants."

"But why should the governess haunt your dollhouse?" asked Charlotte.

Mrs. Smith gazed up at the ceiling. "A pleasant sounding name — Calliope Honeywell," she said as if she had not heard Charlotte's question. "Ca. Lie. Oh. Pee. That's how you say it. A sweet-sounding, musical name, don't you think?"

"My real name is Penelope," Penny interjected. "Pen. Ell. Oh. Pee. I hate it."

"Miss Calliope Honeywell came to stay with us when I was only ten years old," continued Mrs. Smith, still gazing up at the ceiling as if the story she were about to tell them was written up there in the plaster. "She arrived, she stayed, and in a very short time she made my life a sort of hell."

Zibby settled back in her chair and listened. Jude's shoulder touched Zibby's. Zibby felt comforted by her touch. Penny and Charlotte leaned forward to hear better.

"I hated her," Mrs. Smith was saying in a soft voice. "I hated her very much indeed. And so I started trying to get even with her. I began thinking up practical jokes — tried to teach her a few lessons. Maybe everything would have turned out differently if I hadn't felt the need to take revenge on her, because in the end the practical jokes went too far. But they began simply enough, the night I clipped a clothespin onto her beaky old nose to stop the terrible snoring . . ."

The girls listened, rapt and horrified, as Mrs. Smith told her story.

# Chapter 19

## *Primrose (1919)*

After Miss Honeywell's funeral, Primrose lay in bed. She hadn't been able to stop shivering for days. Immediately after she'd heard Miss Honeywell's voice in her head, she'd stopped screaming and started shivering. She had had the presence of mind to run back to the closet and lock herself in. That was where she was when Nanny Shanks came running into the schoolroom and found Miss Honeywell — dead.

Primrose cried out to her from the closet and said the governess had locked her inside. That much was true, after a fashion, but it was the only truth Primrose told about what had happened. She said she'd been locked up in the closet and heard a terrible crash. That was all. Nanny Shanks found Miss Honeywell's keys, but the key for the closet door was not on the ring. So she had to call the menservants to take the door off at the hinges so Primrose could come out.

She was shivering then, and couldn't stop, though Nanny Shanks had built up the fire in the bedroom grate and put her to bed, piling on two extra blankets. Primrose had been in bed until the funeral. She took her meals on trays. But it was hard to eat.

Papa and Mama returned for Christmas to find the house in turmoil. The funeral took place four days later. It hadn't been so terrible. Primrose had never been to a funeral before and wasn't sure what to expect. Moaning and crying and gnashing of teeth as the anguished family of Miss Honeywell wept at the gravesite, maybe. But it seemed Miss Honeywell hadn't had any relatives. The only people who attended the funeral were Primrose's own family and the servants. The service was over quickly after a few short prayers and one song. The minister spoke about how Miss Honeywell had tripped while carrying her water pitcher, how she had fallen and struck her head, shattering the pitcher. He spoke about the sadness of accidental death, but asserted that the Lord alone knew when each of us would be called back to the fold.

Only Primrose knew that it wasn't the Lord who had called Miss Honeywell home to heaven. Only she knew about the last practical joke.

But she didn't tell. She was sorry that Miss Honeywell had died. But she wasn't sorry at all that Miss Honeywell was gone. Gone forever.

Later the same day, after the funeral, Papa let her move back to the nursery, where she would have the babies and Nanny Shanks for company and reassurance. But in bed at night Primrose was alone — alone with her thoughts. It almost seemed too wonderful to be true — that at long last she was really and truly free. Miss Honeywell would never be able to shout at her or lock her in the closet or smack her hands again.

She lay in the dark the night after the funeral, pressing her toes against the hot water bottle, no longer shivering. She felt a little thrill of pleasure.

But suddenly, there in the dark, Primrose's palms began to hurt. They stung — they stung just as if they had been smacked by Miss Honeywell's ruler. Primrose clenched her hands into fists and struck the quilt hard. "You can't do anything to me now!" she whispered.

*Don't be so sure about that, Primrose Parson.*

Primrose held her breath, her palms still stinging. It was the same voice she'd heard in her head after Miss Honeywell fell. She peered around the small bedroom. The babies and Nanny Shanks slept in rooms on either side of her. No one was in her bedroom but her. And yet she knew that voice. "Horrid Old Honeywell!" Her own voice came out a shout.

*That's* Sweet *Miss Honeywell to you, young miss!*

Primrose moaned and ducked beneath the covers.

She heard a noise outside her door — footsteps coming toward her room. She hardly dared to look — afraid to see Miss Honeywell's ghost. But no — it was only Nanny Shanks coming to check on her. "Stay with me, Nanny. Stay with me, please," Primrose begged. And Nanny Shanks settled herself on the chair by Primrose's bed.

"Poor child. Go to sleep now. I'll be here."

Primrose closed her eyes and rubbed her hands against the soft blanket until they didn't hurt anymore. Miss Honeywell was dead and buried, she told herself. She had no power over Primrose anymore. She couldn't do anything to Primrose now. Nothing at all.

But that didn't turn out to be quite true. Primrose discovered very soon after Miss Honeywell's death that indeed the unpleasant governess still had some amount of power. It was the power available to all ghosts. Miss Honeywell had the power to haunt.

Primrose discovered this terrible truth when she next went to play with her dollhouse. She opened the latch and swung the front of the house wide, then settled down with the little doll family. "'Oh, children,'" she made the mama doll say in a sorrowful voice. "'Your papa and I have returned from our travels early because your governess has died. What a shame — but now we must have the funeral.'"

Primrose moved the dolls into the parlor and lay Old Sourpuss in her gray dress on the floor by the little piano. She gathered the other dolls around her. "'May she rest in peace,'" intoned the papa doll. Primrose tipped the other dolls forward to show that they were bowing their heads in prayer. Then she made the girl doll sit at the piano and play a hymn. All the dolls sang along.

"'And now for the burial,'" said the papa doll. And Primrose wrapped Old Sourpuss in the map of Europe, stuffed the whole package into a brown paper bag, and then put on her overcoat. On her way downstairs she met up with Nanny Shanks and the twins, who were on their way out to ride in the sled.

"Come with us, dear girl," invited Nanny Shanks. "We were just coming up to find you."

"Oh, goody," said Primrose, and skipped down the stairs with them. As they rounded the corner of the house on their way to fetch the sleds off the back porch, she dropped the bundle she carried into the trash bin. The garbage collectors would be by in the morning, and that would be the end of Old Sourpuss.

But it wasn't. In the morning after Primrose had watched the garbagemen trundle the bins to their wagon and tip the garbage from the can into the big, stinking pile, she went over to her dollhouse to play. And she had to press her hands against her mouth to hold in her cry — for there in the dollhouse attic was the nasty doll. Primrose reached out her hand, disbelieving her eyes. How could this doll be here? Had Nanny Shanks found it and brought it back? Inside her head she heard a bell ring softly. It sounded like Miss Honeywell's school bell, rung from very far away.

Her palms started stinging as soon as she picked up the doll, and she heard Miss Honeywell's soft, hard voice in her head again.

*Don't think you'll be able to get rid of me, young miss.*

"You can't hurt me," Primrose gasped. "You're dead and gone!"

*I've always said you need governing, my dear. And governing young girls is my greatest strength and pleasure. Dead — yes. But gone? Oh, no, my dear. I shall stay with you forever and ever — until the end of your days.*

# Chapter Twenty

"Till the end of my days!" chortled Mrs. Smith. "But I've had the last laugh, haven't I? I've won!" She beamed at Zibby. "I'd tried and tried to sell that old dollhouse, or give it away — never with any luck. But then the other week I had a sudden inspiration to take the house to the miniature convention in Columbus. Just out of the blue I decided to go. And lucky for me that I did, isn't it? Because there you were."

"But I hadn't been planning to buy a dollhouse at all," murmured Zibby. Something was tickling the back of her mind, some understanding she couldn't quite get hold of. She tried to concentrate, but it slipped away.

"That's why Miss Honeywell can't come back to me," beamed Mrs. Smith. "Because you signed the contract, she's legally bound to you. I wish I'd thought of this way out years ago!"

"I never promised to keep *her!*" snapped Zibby. Her ordinary good manners were forgotten as she stared at Mrs. Smith with dislike. The person before her in the bed seemed less an old, ill woman and more a clever child, a practical joker with a mean streak. Primrose Parson.

Mrs. Smith turned her head feebly on the pillow, but her laugh was loud and excited. "Too bad, honey. You signed the sales contract. You've got her now. And I say good riddance. What a relief it is for me! She has been nothing but bad news. It was because of her that I had to lock up the house. I was deprived of it all through my childhood."

"Why?" asked Jude. "I thought you said you'd begged your parents for a dollhouse."

"Oh, yes, I loved the house. But after Miss Honeywell died, playing with it was no fun. In fact, it was downright dangerous. You see, Sweet Miss Honeywell's ghost made it impossible for me to play with my beloved dollhouse. Whatever I played came out wrong. If I played that the doll children went sledding in the park — my real baby brother and sister were hurt when their sled tipped over. If I played that the doll parents came home from a trip and brought gifts, my real parents came home but found all their luggage — with the gifts they'd bought us inside — had been stolen. Once I played that the nanny doll baked cookies for the dollhouse children, but then my real Nanny Shanks caught her apron on fire and ended up in the hospital."

"That's terrible," said Jude. "But it's exactly the same sort of thing that has been happening to us."

"Well, I am sorry about that," admitted Mrs. Smith. "But I guess a governess always has to have power over someone. And by playing with the house, you're giving her the chance to wield her power. She likes to be in charge. You should lock it up so she can't bother you."

Penny frowned. "So now Zibby has paid all her money for a dollhouse she can't even use? I think it was mean of you to sell her the house, knowing all along that the ghost was there."

"Now, dear, I had no reason to think Miss Honeywell would bother anyone else. It's *me* she has a grudge against, after all. I thought that if the house found a new owner, she'd just go away — to wherever people go when they die. It isn't likely she's in heaven though, not her!"

"Well she hasn't gone anywhere," said Jude fiercely. "She's inside the doll, making trouble for us just as much as she ever did for you."

Charlotte nodded in agreement. "And we never even did anything to her. *You* did."

Mrs. Smith nodded her head weakly on her pillow,

smiling a sly sort of smile. "Yes, yes, that's true. But she has certainly had her revenge. Every time I tried to get rid of the doll or the dollhouse, she returned. It was her way of punishing me, you see? Because I did kill her, though I didn't mean to. I found a way to get back at her though!" Mrs. Smith's giggle was high-pitched, like that of a little girl. Zibby winced. "I couldn't stop her from taking up residence in my dollhouse," Mrs. Smith continued with a laugh. "But I sure could stop myself playing with the dollhouse. And so I did. I packed it all up and I never once played with it again. I sometimes wished I could get my papa to buy me another house, one that wasn't haunted, but that would mean telling him why. I tried to give the dollhouse to my little sister, but it just kept reappearing in my room. Then I tried packing it away to the cellar storeroom — I even locked it inside. But to no avail. There it was again, back in my room."

Zibby and Jude looked at each other, nodding.

"When I was twelve and moved out of the nursery, it appeared in my new bedroom, too," whispered Mrs. Smith. She lifted her head off the pillow briefly, then let if fall back. "Our Sweet Miss Honeywell never did like to be told no, not for any reason."

"Couldn't you have explained to your parents why you wanted the house thrown away? Surely if they knew it was haunted, they wouldn't want it in your house," Charlotte spoke up.

"I didn't want them to know that I was being haunted," explained Mrs. Smith. "I didn't want them to ask why."

"You didn't want anyone to know the real reason she had died," said Zibby harshly. She felt angry at Mrs. Smith. Despite the old woman's feeble appearance and poor health, she felt the presence of a strong, selfish will.

"That's right, my dear." Mrs. Smith winked at Zibby. "I covered my tracks. I dropped that closet key into the river one afternoon when Nanny Shanks took us to the park. And then I took the dollhouse to the backyard that same night and broke it to pieces with a sledgehammer. And yet, what do you know? The key never turned up again, but that house was right back in my room when I woke up. Without a scratch on it, believe it or not."

"Oh, I believe it," said Zibby wryly.

"I left for boarding school when I was twelve, and I thought that at last I'd be rid of the dollhouse," continued Mrs. Smith, glancing away from Zibby to look at the other girls. "But, no. Even there, she found me. The house just appeared in my room at school, and I had a devil of a time explaining to the headmistress where it had come from. We weren't allowed to have toys in our rooms, but the dollhouse wouldn't stay away. My roommates thought it was a wonderful joke I was playing on the headmistress, but of course it wasn't. Finally I hid the house in the closet, behind my dresses."

She winked at the girls, a slow flicker of a wink. "And even when I married, the dollhouse had to come along on my honeymoon. Poor, dear Mr. Smith — he always humored me, though I never told him the story."

"You mean the dollhouse has been with you your *whole* life?" marveled Charlotte.

"Yes, that's right, dear," replied Mrs. Smith, a weak smile flickering on her lips. "It has been an unpleasant reminder of my last practical joke. Maybe a symbol of my guilt? Who knows. But finally, as I said, I had a sudden inspiration. The miniature convention. The sales contract."

"And that's where I came in," said Zibby slowly. "But I wonder why Miss Honeywell would want to stay with me?"

"Oh, I don't think she wanted to stay with you," Mrs. Smith corrected her calmly. "She had to, I believe, because I made you sign the contract. That's what did the trick." Her cool blue gaze was steady. "You were just in the right place at the right time."

Zibby sat silently, trying to figure it all out.

"One thing's been bothering me," Jude said suddenly. "Why did you choose such a low price for the dollhouse when it's worth so much more?"

"I just wanted to get rid of it fast," said Mrs. Smith.

Charlotte spoke up, puzzled. "But how come you

wanted eighty-five dollars and seventy-six cents? I mean, why the seventy-six cents? It's such an odd amount."

Mrs. Smith shrugged. "Oh, I don't know. It seemed like a good price, all of a sudden."

*All of a sudden.* Zibby frowned. A lot of things seemed to have happened all of a sudden. "But that's the point," she said slowly. "How could you know *to the last cent* the amount I had in my pocket that day? I didn't even know myself that I had the extra change in my pocket."

Mrs. Smith shook her head. "Of course I couldn't have known. It's just a coincidence."

Jude gazed at Zibby. "I don't think," she began slowly, "that coincidences happen like that. *Someone* must have known."

Again, the niggling sense of something just beyond her understanding tickled Zibby's mind. A puzzle piece not yet in place.

Penny chimed in, breathless. "Someone?"

And then Zibby knew. "Miss Honeywell!"

Mrs. Smith smiled gaily. "Nonsense! Why would Miss Honeywell choose to let the dollhouse change owners after all this time? No, I was the clever one that day. I've had the last laugh in the end."

*In the end.* Distantly, Zibby heard the bell ringing. It grew louder. It was Miss Honeywell's school bell, she knew now, right inside her head. With the ringing of the bell came a new clarity, as if the governess's unseen hand had dropped the last piece of the puzzle into place.

*The last laugh?* Zibby stared at Mrs. Smith, lying so weakly there in her hospital bed, and then the terrible truth dawned. Zibby shook her head. "I don't think so," she murmured.

"No?"

"No. I don't think it was chance at all that you decided to go to the miniature convention that day. I think it was Miss Honeywell who *made* you go. I think she wanted you to sell the house this time. She knew it was — well, time for a new owner. I think she chose me herself. A ghost could know exactly how much money I had — *you* couldn't know, but *she* did. It wasn't anything to do with your sales contract, Mrs. Smith. Miss Honeywell is haunting me now because —" Zibby hesitated. "Because she knew she didn't want to stay with you much longer."

"Now why would she want a change after all these years?" queried Mrs. Smith. "She said she'd be with me always — till the end of my days, she said — and I fully expected she would . . ."

Mrs. Smith broke off, staring at Zibby in shocked realization. Then she started coughing, gasping for breath between each cough. The nurse rushed in from the hallway and helped Mrs. Smith into a sitting position, thumping her back hard. At last the coughing subsided. The nurse lowered Mrs. Smith back onto her pillows.

Zibby watched as Mrs. Smith slumped sideways on the bed. A little fleck of foam at the corner of her open mouth slid slowly down her chin. The nurse wiped her face.

Mrs. Smith's voice came out as a moan. "You mean — you mean you think she *knew*? You think Miss Honeywell knows I don't have long to live — is that it? She wanted to make sure she had a new little girl to govern?"

Zibby nodded soberly. "I'm afraid that's probably what happened. That would explain why I suddenly wanted to buy a dollhouse I'd had no intention of buying. Why I felt I was looking for something. Why the house cost exactly the amount of money I had that day. Miss Honeywell was manipulating everything."

"She wanted you." Mrs. Smith's voice was only a whisper now. "Because she knew she wouldn't have me much longer." The nurse hovered over her, impatient for the girls to leave. "I suspect she thought you needed governing. She would want a child who was weak."

"Weak?" bristled Jude. "Zibby's healthy and strong."

"I mean emotionally weak, my dear. In turmoil, perhaps. Sad about something, maybe. Sweet Miss Honeywell could always find weak spots, and use them to her advantage."

And Zibby recalled how she had been feeling on

her birthday when she'd bought the dollhouse. Sad because Amy had just moved. Bereft because her dad had just married Sofia. Angry because Nell wanted to look at dollhouses instead of taking her to Sportsmart as promised for the birthday Rollerblades. *Maybe I was a little weak that day,* she thought. *Weak enough, anyway, for Miss Honeywell to choose me for her new girl.*

The nurse motioned for the girls to leave. Zibby reached out impulsively and touched Mrs. Smith's gnarled hand where it lay atop the sheet. There didn't seem to be anything left to say. But Mrs. Smith moaned faintly, "I guess the joke's on me."

# Chapter 21

The girls biked back to Carroway without talking. Charlotte went straight home, Zibby and the Jeffersons pedaled on across town, through the park to Oaktree Lane. Zibby waved good-bye to Penny and Jude at their driveway and sailed down the street to her own house. Her mom wasn't home, but there was a note on the kitchen counter that she had gone out to lunch with Ned Shimizu. They would be back soon. Feeling as if she were walking through a fog, Zibby fixed herself a peanut butter and blueberry jam sandwich and poured a glass a milk. She sat at the kitchen table, staring out the window, thinking about the little girl who had killed her governess so many years ago. She thought about the angry and determined Miss Calliope Honeywell, whose need to wield power and exact revenge had reached out to Primrose from beyond the grave.

Zibby shivered. It was hard to believe that things

like this could really happen. Her dad and mom both had always scoffed at the notion of ghosts. But she had seen Miss Honeywell's power for herself. And now Miss Honeywell, knowing that Primrose did not have long to live, had chosen a new child to govern.

The only thing to do to keep Miss Honeywell from wielding power in her own life, Zibby decided, would be to do as Primrose Parson had done and lock away the dollhouse. The house might follow her around forever, but at least the ghost could not break free. She stood up, resolute. But before she could go upstairs, the phone rang.

It was Jude, and her excited jabbering was unintelligible at first. "Calm down, calm down," said Zibby. "I can't understand a word you're saying!"

"Oh, Zibby, he's okay, my dad's okay! We just had a call from my mom in Kenya, right when Penny and I came in the door. My mom said that Dad was found lying trapped in the bottom of a gorge. He was sure that he'd broken both legs, because he was pinned under a huge boulder, but when the rescue party got him out, he could walk! Can you believe it?" Jude's voice trembled. "Oh, Zibby, it's amazing — he didn't even have any water or food left. He's dehydrated and weak, and has a gigantic bump on the head, but he's going to be just fine!"

"Wow!" cried Zibby, gladness flooding her. "This is *super.*"

"Noddy says it's a miracle, and Nana is dancing around the house for joy. Mom says that since he's going to be okay, they're going to stay on and get back to their work with the new hospital, but they'll come home for Christmas for sure. I'm just so excited, I don't even care that that's still months away. Just as long as my dad's safe. That's all that matters."

Zibby agreed. She talked to Penny, too, then hung up and sat at the table with a smile on her face, happy and relieved.

A tapping on the kitchen door made her jump. She ran to the door, and there was Charlotte. She looked different. It took a second before Zibby realized that the bandage on her forehead was gone.

"Your head," Zibby said, opening the screen door and letting Charlotte into the kitchen.

"I know," said Charlotte, touching her head in wonderment. "Isn't it amazing?" She twirled around the kitchen. "As soon as I got home, the bandage just sort of suddenly dropped off. And the gash is so much better, my mom couldn't believe it. She says she's going to take me to the doctor tomorrow. But you can already tell that the scar will hardly show once the stitches are out."

"That's amazing," said Zibby slowly.

Charlotte pirouetted around the kitchen. "And there's something else amazing, Zib! We just had a call from the police that all our things have been found.

They were in big trash bags at the town dump, can you believe it? They're not hurt at all. We just have to drive over and collect them and clean them up. My mom and dad are doing that right now. But I wanted to come here to tell you. It seems like our luck is taking a turn for the better."

"Yeah," agreed Zibby, and told Charlotte about Mac Jefferson's rescue in Kenya. "All this good luck, so quickly — it's a little bit strange, don't you think?"

Charlotte bit her lip. "Too good to be true, you mean? You know, I bet it's something to do with Miss Honeywell. Do you think she's sorry for her nastiness or something?"

Zibby considered this. "Well, she should be. But why should she suddenly change?"

The phone rang again before Charlotte could answer, and Zibby ran to answer. *What now?* she was thinking. Astonishingly, the call brought more good news. It was Amy on the phone, saying that her dad was out of the hospital early. He was walking nearly as good as new, she reported. He still had his cast on, but didn't need to lie in traction. "The doctors say he can come home!" She laughed. "And so he's going to drive me down to visit you after all. I can come the weekend after next. Will that be all right?"

Zibby assured her it would be wonderful. She hung up and turned to Charlotte. "Remember what Jude said to Mrs. Smith about coincidences not just happening? Well, this is definitely not coincidence either, I bet." She told her cousin about Amy's dad. "Isn't it just too weird that everything is turning out okay — all at once?"

Charlotte nodded. "It's weird to think that Miss Honeywell would suddenly turn nice."

Then Zibby's mom and Ned Shimizu walked into the kitchen together. "Hello, girls, what's up?" Ned asked jovially. Then Nell said hello, breaking off abruptly and reaching out to touch Charlotte's head. "My goodness, Char," she said in surprise. "This has certainly healed fast."

Zibby and Charlotte exchanged a glance. Zibby reached out and caught her mom's hand. She turned it over and inspected the wrist. It was just as she thought. Only a faint red mark where the burn had been.

Nell looked, too, and her laugh sounded puzzled. "Well, you and I must be pretty healthy," she said to Charlotte. "Good genes or immune systems or something!"

As soon as Nell and Ned had gone out of the room, Zibby reached for the phone. "I'm going to call Mrs. Smith at the hospital," she told Charlotte. "I think she'd like to know that Miss Honeywell is fixing all the trouble she caused."

When the receptionist answered, Zibby asked to

speak to the head nurse in intensive care. She was connected promptly, but when she asked for Mrs. Smith, there was a silence.

"Are you one of the children who just visited her this morning?"

"Yes," said Zibby. "I just wanted to talk to her for a minute."

"Well, I'm afraid that won't be possible," the nurse said slowly.

"You mean she's not feeling any better?"

There was a silence, and then the nurse's voice came over the line, gentle and solemn. "I'm afraid that shortly after you left today, Mrs. Smith passed away."

# Chapter 22

"Passed away?" cried Zibby, and Charlotte gasped. "You mean she *died?*"

"Yes. I'm sorry, but her heart was very weak."

"Did we — I mean, did our visit somehow —" Zibby could barely ask the question.

The nurse's voice was firm and reassuring. "Absolutely not. My dear, Mrs. Smith was very old, and her heart was just plain worn out. The doctors knew she didn't have long to live. It was only a matter of time. Your visit made her last morning more pleasant. She had been very eager to see you."

"Well," murmured Zibby. "Well, I just hope —"

"It's hard when a friend dies," said the nurse. And Zibby agreed, although Primrose Parson Smith had not been a friend, exactly. But she had mattered.

Zibby called Jude and Penny. "I know you guys must be celebrating up a storm over there," she said, "but I really think you ought to come over. Charlotte's already here. And — I just heard that Mrs. Smith died."

"Oh, no! We'll be right over," said Jude.

Zibby and Charlotte didn't have long to wait till they heard the patter of Jude's and Penny's sandals on the front porch. Zibby opened the door even before the girls rang the bell. Silently they all walked upstairs to Zibby's room and settled on the floor.

"A lot of weird things are going on," Zibby said solemnly.

"Well we already knew that," said Penny.

"But at least these weird things are good things," said Charlotte. "Like Mac Jefferson being found safe. Like the police finding all our stuff at the dump."

"And your head, Charlotte," added Penny. "And your mom's wrist, too, Zibby. That's all weird, but at least it's weird in a good way this time."

"I think it's also weird that Mrs. Smith died just after we saw her today," said Jude. "Because it was just after we came home from seeing her that all the good stuff started happening."

"Even Amy's dad's leg is much better," Zibby told them. "And he's bringing her here to visit next weekend. It's all almost too good to be true. I can't think why Miss Honeywell should suddenly turn out to be nice. Unless —"

"What?" asked Penny.

"Unless she's just glad that Primrose Parson is dead."

Jude looked mystified. "I'm not sure that makes sense. You mean she's celebrating?"

Zibby looked at the dollhouse. It was still locked up. She reached for the latch and unhooked it. She swung open the two sides of the house. "It seems to me Miss Honeywell should be gone now. I mean, since Primrose Parson is dead, her governess doesn't need to haunt the dollhouse to get revenge. She can deal with Primrose right in heaven — or wherever it is that ghosts go."

"But remember, Zibby, Miss Honeywell herself engineered the dollhouse sale. She *wanted* the house to have a new owner. She *needed* a new girl because she knew Primrose Parson was going to die. Why should she leave now?"

"Maybe she changed her mind," said Zibby. "She must have changed her mind about a lot of things, or else why would she suddenly start fixing all the things she made go wrong in the first place?"

Zibby and the girls sat there mulling it over in front of the old dollhouse. Then a little sound from the dollhouse made them all stiffen. It was a small rustling sound — the sound Zibby had heard before and once attributed to mice. She didn't believe in mice now. She believed in ghosts.

Zibby knelt before the dollhouse. She listened for bells, she waited for her hands to sting — but there was nothing. And yet — and yet there was something.

Did the other girls feel it, too? Jude slid off the bed and came to sit next to Zibby. The beads at the ends of her many braids clicked comfortingly as she bumped Zibby's shoulder. "What is it? What is it now?"

"I heard something," whispered Charlotte. "Did you?"

"I heard it, too," said Penny.

Zibby looked into the empty dollhouse schoolroom. "Miss Honeywell?" she called out softly. "Are you there?"

A giggle. A rustle of petticoats. All in Zibby's head? Or could the others hear it, too?

Zibby turned to Jude. "Did you hear that?"

Jude shook her head. "No," she whispered. "I don't hear anything, but there's a sort of chill in the room. Something — do you feel it?"

Zibby nodded. Then she heard it, what she had been fearing — and almost waiting for at the same time. A voice in her head.

*I'm here now. I want to stay with you.*

A voice, but higher and lighter, now. A girl's voice.

Zibby heard again the rustle from the dollhouse. She held her breath and peered into the other rooms. There were dolls lying on the floors of the rooms. The nasty-faced doll lay in a pile with the others. She had not moved at all.

But one of the other dolls had moved. The girl doll in the blue silk dress, her brown braids lying neatly over each shoulder, now sat neatly on the living room couch.

Zibby slowly reached her hand into the dollhouse living room and lifted the doll. It seemed to shift under her fingers and she nearly dropped it. But she didn't, and brought it out into her bedroom.

*How could a room on a bright summer's day be haunted?* Zibby wondered. But it felt as if the air itself had thickened. As if a storm were brewing. The other three girls leaned forward to see the girl doll in the blue dress.

"Miss Honeywell?" whispered Zibby.

*No, silly girl. Don't you recognize me?*

Zibby dropped the doll onto the rug. She heard a girlish chortle in her head.

"Listen," Zibby said in a shaky voice. "Miss Honeywell, you don't have to haunt us now. Primrose is gone. She's dead now. You'd better go off to — to heaven, I guess — and look for her there. I'm sure she still needs you to govern her. But I don't need you. Go away!"

*Don't you know who I am?*

"Did you hear that?" cried Zibby. "Did you hear what she said?"

"No, what?" shrieked Penny.

"She asked if I knew who she was."

"Who is she?" breathed Charlotte. "Who are you?" she asked the little doll.

"I know who you are," said Jude suddenly. "You're Primrose Parson!"

*Now that's a girl with a head on her shoulders,* said the voice in Zibby's head.

"You mean you are *Primrose*? You're Mrs. Smith?" asked Zibby wildly. "But — you can't be. I mean, we just saw you in the hospital. I mean, you're dead!"

*But I want to be a girl again.*

"Oh, no you don't! No way! Not in my dollhouse, you can't," said Zibby.

"What's she saying, Zibby?" cried Charlotte. "I can't hear anything."

"Me neither," whispered Penny. "And I don't want to. I want to go home."

"No, wait," said Jude. She reached for Zibby's hand and held it. "Primrose?" She addressed the little doll still lying on the floor. "Why are you here?"

*I told you, I want to be a girl again! I never had a chance to play with this dollhouse when I was a child. Miss Honeywell saw to that. I begged my father for it, and he got it for me, but what good did it ever do me to have it since I couldn't play with it? So I'm going to live in it now.*

"I can hear her, Zibby!" shouted Jude. "Listen, you guys, hold hands with Zibby. Somehow Zibby's the one she talks through, but if you touch Zibby, you can hear her, too!"

Charlotte grabbed Zibby's other hand. Penny tentatively took up Jude's. Then she linked hands with

Charlotte. The four girls sat in a circle in front of the dollhouse with the little girl doll on the floor in the center of the circle.

Zibby couldn't believe any of this was happening. She could feel Charlotte's hand sweating in her own. Zibby spoke to the doll, to the ghost of Primrose Parson. "I'll lock up the house just as you did, and I'll never open it again," she threatened. "You'll be stuck in there, just as Miss Honeywell was. I don't want any ghosts around here."

*But that's not fair,* whined the voice of Primrose Parson. *Miss Honeywell was the one who played mean tricks. I'm the one who made everything all right again. I undid all her mischief. You girls should be thanking me — goodness, I'd think you'd be* inviting *me to stay instead of threatening to lock me up. After all I've just done for you!*

Penny trembled. "I can hear her! I can hear her right in my head!"

Zibby looked around at the other girls, then addressed the doll in the blue dress. "Okay, Primrose," she said. She couldn't imagine calling the doll Mrs. Smith. Mrs. Smith was the old woman in the hospital. This — the voice, anyway — was clearly a girl about their own ages. "Okay, let's just suppose that I let you stay in the dollhouse. What about Miss Honeywell? I'm surprised you would want to live in the same house with her again. That didn't work out too well the first time, remember."

*But she isn't here,* came the ghost's reply. *I looked for her, and she's not around. That's why I was able to undo all the trouble she caused. She doesn't seem to be here to stop me. I bet she's gone searching for me! Ha-ha — that's a laugh. And here I am taking her place.*

The girls looked at each other.

*Please let me stay,* wheedled Primrose. *We can have fun. I can even help you —*

"Help me with what?" demanded Zibby. "I don't need help — or I didn't until you sold me a haunted dollhouse."

*I'm sure there must be all sorts of things a ghost can do — good things, I mean, not the sort of things Miss Honeywell did.* Primrose's voice in the girls' heads held a note of desperation. *I know! I can help with your schoolwork, for one thing. After all, I've lived much longer than you and I'm very well educated. Goodmont Academy, unlike today's schools, was a very rigorous academic environment.*

"Hmm," said Zibby doubtfully. "I don't know about this. But . . ." She glanced at the other girls. "Do you happen to know any French? That's my hardest subject."

*Do I indeed!* said Primrose Parson, and then added in French: *Je parle français très bien!* She giggled. *Also Latin, Italian, and a little bit of German. And I'm wonderful with geography, too. I finally did manage to learn the names of all the rivers in Europe. Shall I tell you? Would you like to write them down now or —*

"Later," Zibby said firmly.

*Oh, good, then there will be a later! Thank you, thank you!*

Zibby couldn't believe she was sitting here talking to the ghost of the very same woman they had visited at the hospital that morning. Was she going to wake up and find all this was only a dream? All of it — this ghost, Miss Honeywell, the dollhouse — even Penny and Jude? What if she woke up and found that Amy still lived down the street, and none of this had happened?

"She knows Italian, Zibby," Charlotte spoke up. "I suppose she could teach you so you can talk to people if you go visit your dad."

"I think you should let her stay," Penny said eagerly. She seemed to be over her earlier fear. "I think Primrose is just a girl who needs some friends. Maybe she can even be in our club."

"Let's not rush into things," Charlotte said nervously.

Jude looked doubtful, too. "Well, it's up to Zibby, really. It's her dollhouse — and it's her ghost."

And Zibby realized that she wouldn't want this all to have been a dream. As weird as it all was, she wanted this to be her life now, with these new friends, and a club, and even this ghost.

*So, is it settled then?* asked Primrose Parson. *Because if so, then I'd very much like to sleep in the blue bedroom. But I'll need some new curtains of course. And the dollhouse is terribly shabby. I hope you'll fix it up, girls. A good cleaning, and some nice fur-*

*nishings. How about some pictures on these bare walls? And what about a plant? I'd dearly love some greenery around here.*

Zibby sighed. Having this ghost around was going to be trouble, one way or another, she could see it already. No sooner did Primrose Parson move in than she was asking for gifts!

*I'm not the only one who likes gifts,* came Primrose Parson's thin voice in Zibby's head, just as though she had read Zibby's thoughts. *I think you'll like yours as much as I'll like mine!*

"My gifts?" Puzzled, Zibby swung around to look, but there were no presents. And yet footsteps were coming up the stairs.

"Zibby?" called Nell's voice. "I think we have a mystery."

Zibby ran to open the bedroom door, and there was her mom, with Ned Shimizu right behind her. Nell was carrying a large box.

"I found this on the porch just now when we arrived home, and the tag says it's for you. A late birthday present, maybe? But I can't think who it could be from. At first I thought maybe your dad, but no, this box didn't come through the mail."

The girls gathered around to watch as Zibby opened the box — and gasped at the brand-new, shiny, purple, pink, and black Rollerblades that lay within.

"They're perfect," said Zibby wonderingly, lifting

the gleaming in-line skates from the box and running her hands over the row of rubber wheels. "Exactly what I wanted."

"And look," said Charlotte, lifting a layer of tissue paper. "Knee pads and wrist guards!"

"I just wish we knew who to thank," Nell said, leaving the room.

"I know who to thank," Zibby whispered, and she went over to the dollhouse. Now the girl doll was sitting at the table in the dining room.

"I guess maybe it will work out for us, Primrose Parson," she told the doll. "You'll live in the dollhouse and I won't lock it up — for now. I don't know much about ghosts, and I sure didn't like the first ghost who was in this house. You'll need to show me I can trust you."

*Oh, you can trust me. It will work out fine.* The painted smile seemed to widen, and Zibby felt a shiver tingle at the back of her neck despite the warmth of the summer evening and the happiness of having the new Rollerblades at last. She reached for Jude's and Penny's hands. Charlotte reached for Penny's other hand. They all heard Primrose Parson's next words.

*We will all be friends. And I will stay with you forever and ever —*

Where had they heard that before?

*— forever and ever . . . till the end of your days . . .*

Jude squeezed Zibby's hand. "Don't worry. We'll be with you that long, too."

Zibby squeezed back. "Good," she said shakily. "I have a feeling I'm going to need all the help I can get!"

—*forever and ever . . . till the end of your days . . .*

# *Dollhouse Furnishings You Can Make*

After it was decided that Primrose would be allowed to stay in the dollhouse, the girls set to work cleaning it up for her. They went to Mrs. Howell's shop in Fennel Grove and bought new wallpaper with patterns of tiny flowers for the bedrooms. Charlotte and Penny carefully applied it to the walls with a thin glue. Zibby and Jude set to work fashioning a few tiny potted plants for the dollhouse. Zibby used the caps from her tube of toothpaste and from Nell's tube of hair conditioner. She hoped her mom wouldn't mind, but figured she was too preoccupied with Ned to notice. Jude filled the caps with little balls of modeling clay from Zibby's art box, then Zibby pulled sprigs from a bouquet of flowers Ned had brought for her mom. The little dried flowers were perfect. They were called baby's breath, Jude told her. Zibby stabbed their stems into the clay, then lined the little plants up on the desk. "They're adorable," Penny declared when she saw them. "They look really real!"

And Primrose Parson, when they brought the plants to the dollhouse, agreed.

What you'll need to make houseplants for your own dollhouse:

caps from toothpaste tubes

modeling clay or Play-Doh
(even little balls of dough made from soft bread will do!)

sprigs of small dried flowers

tiny leaves

1. Roll the clay or dough into little balls and press into the caps.
2. Add the flowers and leaves you've collected.
3. Display the potted plants on tables and bookshelves near the windows of your dollhouse. **Warning**: Don't water the plants! The clay needs to dry out and harden.

# About the Author

Kathryn Reiss has written numerous novels for young readers including *Time Windows* and *Dreadful Sorry,* which are both available as Scholastic paperbacks.

Ms. Reiss holds an MFA in creative writing from the University of Michigan. She lives in Oakland, California, with her husband, two sons, and new baby daughter.

Don't miss

# THE GHOST IN THE DOLLHOUSE

## *The Headless Bride* #2

Soon Ned and Laura-Jane returned from the kitchen. They walked into the dining room, Ned looking somber, Laura-Jane looking relieved. And because Nell's eyes were closed, she missed seeing what the others saw: One of the two chandeliers — the one hanging from the ceiling almost directly above Nell's bent head — began to sway. It trembled for a moment as if set in motion by its own private earthquake, then slowly began to swing back and forth with a tinkling of glass pendants. Zibby, Laura-Jane, and Ned all gazed upward in horrified fascination.

"What's making it do that?" whispered Laura-Jane, hands pressed against her cheeks. Zibby released her mom's head and stood, open-mouthed, as Ned grabbed a chair and jumped up on it to try to grab hold of the chandelier.

"Don't stop, Zib," murmured Nell in a sleepy voice. "That was so wonderful . . ." She opened her eyes and smiled, but the smile changed to a look of terror as she looked up just in time to see the nearest chandelier shake loose from the ceiling. In a flash, Zibby tackled her mom sideways, knocking her off her chair to the floor and landing on top of her just as the chandelier crashed down onto the table — right onto the place mat where Nell had laid her head. Sharp shards of glittering glass sliced into the air, and the heavy chain shattered the popcorn bowl and sent fluffy white kernels bouncing onto the floor.

In the shocked silence that followed, as Nell groaned and shifted under Zibby's weight, Zibby knew the danger to her mom was not over. It seemed that Laura-Jane was contrite for her part in all the trouble, and Todd would soon be in police custody — a threat to no one but himself. But cruel Miss Honeywell still meant business.